HARD TO BREAK

DENVER KODIAKS
BOOK 3

PIPER LAWSON

Content editing by Becca Mysoor
Line and copy editing by Cassie Robertson
Proofreading by Devon Burke
Cover design by Emily Wittig

HARD TO TAKE

DENVER KODIAKS #3

My teammate's little sister is all I've ever wanted. Now I'll do whatever it takes to keep her.

I've loved her in secret for years. I kept her safe from the sidelines, even though I knew better.

Everyone knows me as the good times guy, the player with a million dollar smile. Never taking anything too seriously.

Except for her.

She's my end game. I'd sacrifice anything for Brooke, but my choices risk my team and the future of the Denver Kodiaks.

The past never forgets and I'm about to play for my life.

The world might count me out, but I won't go down without a fight. I have my team at my back and the girl of my dreams on the line.

Everyone's going to learn I'm hard to break.

Hard to Break is a pro basketball romance with banter, spice, and all the swoony vibes! It's the third and final book in the Denver Kodiaks series. Miles and Brooke's addictive story begins in Hard to Fake and continues in Hard to Take.

TROPES:
🏀brother's best friend
🤍roommates
🏀pro athlete hero
🤍he's always wanted her
🏀cinnamon roll hero
🤍sassy heroine
🏀college crush
🤍secret dating

For every strong woman who wants
someone to show her the meaning of "little spoon."

HOOPSNEWS UPDATE: BRAWL OUTSIDE KODIAK STADIUM LEAVES MORE QUESTIONS

1

———

BROOKE

The back passenger window of the Range Rover sticks to my neck. My jacket is bunched at the small of my back.

A cramp threatens to seize my calf, which is trapped awkwardly against the seat.

The tension I'm most aware of is the one deep in my stomach, thrumming between my thighs.

"Listen to me, Brooke. This thing is going to detonate in your face." My mom's voice over the phone line carries a hint of static.

I try to shift, less than half my brain on the conversation because a six-four-and-a-half pro basketball player is on top of me with one hand tangled in my hair and the other spanning my ass. His lips trail lazily down my throat like it's his job and he's getting paid by the minute.

This wasn't the plan exactly. I didn't start today with "steamy sweat session in the parking garage of Kodiaks Arena" on my Bingo card, but I can't seem to shut it down.

"We need to do damage control," Mom goes on.

She might as well be on another planet.

Miles drags my sweater up above my breasts. My hips lift to help him, providing the most delicious friction. He hisses out a breath and looks up at me with devious blue eyes before ducking back to kiss a line up my stomach.

"Blame Kevin," I say into the phone. "He started it."

Ow! Smooth lips are replaced by sharp teeth in a fleeting warning.

Guess Miles doesn't like hearing Kevin's name.

My ex in college not only cheated on me and left cocaine in my room for my sorority sisters to find, but he'd put the blame on me. Miles, acting out of loyalty to my brother, had beaten the crap out of Kevin and told him never to come near me again.

Evidently, Kevin's memory is wearing off, because he thinks he isn't done with me—or with Miles.

Miles Garrett has loomed large in my life for years. Back in college, I wasn't that into basketball players, but my brother's friend was different. Sure, he was gorgeous. Tall, with sparkling blue eyes that seemed to laugh at himself as much as at you. But he was also the guy you'd want to have your back.

My brother trusted him. His teammates did.

When you were with him, you felt accepted.

Right now, "accepted" isn't what springs to mind as his fingers trace beneath the waistband of my pants, the friction lighting up my nerves with want.

Miles's thumb rubs across the button, and I arch to get closer.

He smells like his shower, clean and addictive.

"It's not that simple." Mom's still there, trying to tell me something. "What matters is the story, what people perceive."

It's hard to think anything is genuinely terrible when Miles's fingers are deftly working free the button on my pants, unzipping my fly.

"People don't need a story if they have the truth," I manage.

The truth is, Kevin was waiting for Miles to get to the Kodiaks' arena last night. While Miles did hit Kevin, it was only after Kevin goaded him, baited him, and threw the first punch. Miles had been doing his best to avoid a confrontation. Dozens of bystanders with phones caught it.

"And yet every piece of footage only shows Miles Garrett, pro basketball player, hitting an upstanding community member."

New tension has my stomach flexing.

I hate the thought of the world being persuaded once again of Kevin's side of the story. This time, it's not only me at risk.

It's Miles. He's having the season of his career so far, and he doesn't just want it—he needs it. He has people he's looking out for, like his Grams.

After we got home, he was still edgy, still angry. I asked him what Kevin had confronted him with and he wouldn't confide in me. When he fell asleep, he was restless.

It's easy to forget he has any vulnerabilities when he's big and strong, filling the car, his oversized thumb pressing into my hip.

"We'll handle it." I sound confident. Years of rehearsing will do that for you.

"Will you?" Mom scoffs. A car door slams somewhere in the VIP parking section. She doesn't approve, which I can bolster myself against, but it's her disbelief that it could ever work that feeds my own doubt.

We've only just come out publicly and the Kodiaks were at each other's throats. They brokered a truce for the sake of the team. We're in uncharted waters.

Miles's fingers slip between my legs, playing

through the thin fabric of my thong. Pleasure floods me like the sweetest drug.

"You're not in love with him, are you?" Mom demands.

Her words make my breath catch.

I can't remember wanting to be somewhere that he isn't, getting through an entire day without joking with him, how I ever stayed warm an entire winter in Denver without those blazing eyes setting my soul on fire.

Is that love?

Does it change everything if it is?

"I have to go," I manage.

"He's not ready for what's going to happen," she warns. "And he'll drag you down with him."

The idea of him losing everything is a sharper pain than anything from the cramp in my leg or the nip of his teeth.

I click off, dropping the phone onto the seat and blowing a piece of hair out of my face. "My mom says hi."

Miles pulls away to look down at me, eyes crinkling. "That all she said? You don't normally grind your teeth when I'm trying to fuck you."

Since we started this thing, we haven't put words to our feelings. It's still new even though I've known Miles for years. He's been part of my world for what feels like forever but always on the periphery. Teasing and taunting.

Miles cares, but that's different from having someone by your side to see you through the worst times, and the best ones.

Before I can respond, his phone goes off too.

"Chloe," we say at the same time.

"You have to go," I say.

He curses. "Pick this up later?"

I'm as reluctant as he is. It's almost as if we can forget our problems if we're touching.

But there going to be fallout. We'll have to deal with it.

"Is there anything you want to tell me about the fight?" I ask.

I haven't been able to kick the feeling that something is wrong since yesterday before the game. Like Miles has been holding out on me.

He blinks. "No. Your mom didn't have anything else to say?"

I replay her words in my mind. "Nothing." I press a quick kiss to his mouth. "Good luck."

MILES

"I RESCHEDULED a root canal for this, and you know what? I'd rather be at the dentist," James declares.

The owner of the Kodiaks occupies the head of the conference table. His hands are steepled, fingers manicured.

I'm on the side near the window, Chloe two seats down. At the other end of the table, opposite James, is Harlan, the GM.

I got called to the principal's office a handful of times in high school. The first was for a prank we pulled on our coach. Another time was for arguing with a teacher. In both instances, Grams listened to me vent about it and smiled at me after.

The third time, Grams wasn't smiling. She told me I knew better and gave me a talking to and reminded me what was at stake—my future.

I always got what it meant to have a future even if I didn't have a clear picture of it in my mind. I wanted my life to be better—to be accepted, to know where I fit and have people who had my back no matter what.

"I hope we all know why we're here." James is really taking this principal thing to heart, only it's impossible to forget the stakes are far higher than a suspension.

"We're here because some deluded fan picked a

fight with our starting shooting guard," Chloe weighs in.

I cut her a grateful look.

Going into this, I wasn't sure where the battle lines lay. I might not be a strategist like Brooke, but I know enough to realize that's what this meeting is— a battle.

Is it possible the head of PR is on my side?

"That's not what's all over the internet." James pulls out his phone, scrolling through whatever's on his screen. If it's possible, his frown deepens. "The accusations are damaging."

Harlan clears his throat. "What's most important is the record of this basketball team. We're here to win games."

"You have the luxury of caring about the record. I have to care about the name." James jerks out of his chair and paces the front of the room.

Fifty bucks says he kicks the trash can by the door.

The voice in my head might be cracking jokes, but this is serious. The Kodiaks won a championship last year and our chance to win another is slipping through our fingers. I didn't need to read the sports news today to see our seventh-place ranking, down in recent weeks thanks to me and Jay fighting, and now Kevin decides to vent his frustrations in my face on the team's doorstep.

It's not a good look for us.

Growing up with my parents splitting and letting me fall through the cracks of their bitter war taught me not to take relationships for granted.

Through hard work and luck, my life became a regular rotation of games and practices, hanging with my guys, spending time with whatever girls were easy to be around when I wanted it. Now, every part of my existence has been dialed up.

Basketball. My family.

Brooke.

I moved her in with me when she needed to save some cash while she was building her own career because I knew firsthand what it felt like to need someone and not have them there.

The weeks I spent trying to resist her up close after years of doing it from a distance were pure torture.

Now, I wake up with Brooke beside me, getting to hold her, to laugh with her, to touch her. Feeling wanted, accepted.

It's new.

It's addictive.

She's the best part of my world and I hold my breath as if I'm waiting for it all to shatter.

There's a knock at the door, and Jay walks in. "Sorry I'm late."

I straighten in my chair at my friend and team captain's appearance.

He scans the table and the available seats. It's only a second but feels like a year before he chooses one near Harlan.

Who invited him—Harlan? James? Maybe even Chloe?

"We're here to decide how to move forward in the wake of the assault in front of the arena," James goes on.

"On Miles," Chloe says smoothly.

"Excuse me?" James's eyes narrow, but Chloe only taps her pencil on her tablet.

"If there was an assault, it was on Miles."

"None of the security cameras had an angle that would show that, and oddly, none of the fan videos do either."

"Then if we can't prove it, we call it an altercation."

James curses. "The other man could lay charges."

"He won't," I cut in.

He turns to me for what feels like the first time. "How do you know?"

Because I know what he did back in college.

"I just know."

"Well, thank you, Garrett, for bringing your crystal fucking ball to the meeting."

"He could have already. He hasn't." Harlan's answer is more defensible. "But we have to respond somehow."

"We close ranks." Chloe spreads her hands. "Miles Garrett is our all-star candidate. We support him. We put out a team statement saying we don't condone what happened, particularly on team property, but he didn't start it. It ended promptly with the help of security before the police arrived. Anyone who was there can vouch for him."

"That's up for discussion." James stops pacing next to the window.

"Which part?" she asks.

"The all-star part."

His words suck the oxygen from the room.

Getting the nod from my team was an honor I never expected but appreciated more than I could say. If the Kodiaks withdraw their support, formally or informally, there goes my chance of getting to represent the organization—a chance that's supposed to be announced in the next few days.

My sponsorship deal was inked on the assumption that I'd get seriously considered, if not selected. If the Kodiaks back away, my sponsor will cut ties. The security I want for Grams could evaporate. Everything I've been building since I started in the league, since I started playing basketball, could come crashing down.

"Second option—we distance ourselves from this." James's gaze lands on me, and I take "this" to mean "me." "Garrett is on leave pending a full investigation where he puts his fucking head down and does not appear on the court or the property or otherwise in anything with a Kodiaks logo on it until we are well and fully satisfied this 'altercation' was a mistake."

Every cell of my body hurts. It's partly the idea of losing the chance to be an all-star, but more than that, being ripped from my team—the guys, the routines, the job. It's who I am. It's my family.

Harlan shifts in his seat. "We can spin ourselves around in circles trying to protect the image of this team, but the team's value comes not from a spotless reputation, but from winning. We finish tenth in the standings, no one cares how clean our noses are."

I'm usually the guy who breaks up fights, not starts them. The one who keeps the peace, and right now, we need some peace.

"I get that you're concerned," I interject. "And if I made things worse for the Kodiaks, I apologize. It won't happen again."

James grunts. "It's a little late. The best way to

move forward cleanly is to distance ourselves from this. An assault—altercation—with a fan—"

"He wasn't a fan," Jay cuts in for the first time. Every head swivels toward him. "He's a grade-A asshole."

James consults his phone again, his expression doubtful. "Ivy League law school. Multigenerational family firm. Doesn't exactly scream troublemaker."

"Not everything worth knowing is on the internet," Jay responds evenly.

Chloe blinks at him in surprise.

Since he found out about me and Brooke, our relationship has been rocky. We agreed to put the worst of it aside to finish out the season, but it's no sure thing that he'd have my back now.

James looks around the faces at the table. I always pictured him as a rich kid who grew up with expensive tastes and a craving for the spotlight. More often than not, guys like that are the ones who decide our fates.

I can see the moment he realizes he's outnumbered.

"Draft the release," he barks to Chloe. "It was a misunderstanding. The parties were known to one other. It has been settled, and Garrett has since apologized for his role."

I exhale the air I've been holding in for what feels like an hour.

My hand under the table relaxes a little.

There's nothing to fight.

James is out the door in a second, Harlan a few moments later.

"Thanks, man," I say to Jay.

He jerks his chin. "Yeah."

The friendship we had is still a long way from being healed. I wish I knew how to fix it.

Chloe reaches for her phone. "Well played." She nods to me, but her gaze lingers on Jay. "Both of you."

Jay doesn't smile. "Don't get too excited. Like we agreed, the team needs Garrett if we're going to make the playoffs, and Kevin's a piece of shit." He rises from his seat.

"Miles? We're going to need evidence." Our head of PR gathers her things, tucking folders and tablets under one arm.

I frown. "Of what?"

Chloe pauses at the door, turning smoothly. "Your apology to Kevin."

2

BROOKE

Dear Ms. Ellis,

As we are currently conducting our investigation into our corporate practices, we kindly request that you remove any content posted for Vivaro to date and return any merchandise you have received.

Sincerely,
Vivaro Management

"Do they teach asshole in school?" Nova puffs as she reads over my shoulder.

"The time slot clashed with music appreciation." I slip the phone into my pocket and jump over a log on the trail.

I asked Nova to go on a midday hike because I

needed some girl time. Today there's barely any snow, but the grass is long dead and pine needles crunch under my stomping feet. The sun slants through the trees, hinting at spring. Not sure who it thinks it's fooling—it's not even February and so not going to be spring for a hot minute.

Thanks to the Vivaro email, I'm not getting paid anytime soon. Of course, the one brand I was building a collaboration with turned out to be taking advantage of other smaller creators.

It was always going to be a risk to stand up for the other creators who asked for my support. Now, not only has Vivaro put a hold on any future work together, but other companies I've talked with aren't responding.

Still, thanks to Miles, I have a roof over my head and was spared going to my mom or brother for a handout that would come with opinions and strings.

Which is nowhere near the only perk of living with him.

"How are things with you and Miles?" Nova asks.

"We might have set a new record for orgasms," I offer, my mind offering up a few of those extremely satisfying encounters.

Nova's eyes dance. "You've hooked up on every horizontal surface in that condo?"

"Some of the vertical ones too."

She laughs. "It's more than that though. I see how he looks at you."

The hairs on my neck and arms lift, and it's not from the cold. The tingling starts deep in my stomach when I picture Miles's handsome face, hear his voice, imagine him near.

I shoot her a look. "It's new, and I get the sense he wants it to be easy. Not just him and me, but all of it. Maybe it should be, but I can't help thinking about the pitfalls.

"My mom keeps telling me it's a huge mistake. I get comments daily on my social profiles telling me how wrong I am for dating him. But at least Jay doesn't look at Miles like he wants to murder him when they're in the same room, so that's progress."

My brother and I talked a few days ago, but it's not like all the wounds are immediately healed.

Nova nudges my shoulder. "People don't like change. It's threatening to them, and no matter how beautiful a new reality might be, they only see the risk."

I turn that over as we continue down the trail, the sun filtering through the trees and warming us.

"The team decided to keep supporting Miles as an all-star nominee, but the timing of that run-in with Kevin was the worst possible. I can't help feeling I'm missing part of the story." I chew my lip.

"Miles didn't tell you what Kevin said to him?"

"Just that he owed Kevin something, then Kevin hit him." I shake my head. "Somehow the handful of videos posted online show Miles throwing the first punch, and conveniently, no one seems to show Kevin shoving him first."

"You think Kevin was jealous?"

"No," I decide. "I saw him recently and didn't give him what he wanted. I think he needed someone to take it out on. Kevin has a temper but he'll get it under control. I just feel awful for Miles. I brought this to him."

"I'm pretty sure the fact that Miles chose to beat up Kevin back in college wasn't your fault," Nova reminds me.

I feel a hit of gratitude.

"More than one commentor has made the connection that I went to school with Kevin and we dated. They're trying to make me out to be the bad guy. What if I am?"

I thought I knew pressure from growing up on social media, with the mother and brother I have, but being with Miles is bringing an extra layer of scrutiny.

"You're no villain, Brooke Ellis. I will fight anyone who says otherwise."

My lips twitch. "Thanks, but no thanks. The last

thing I need is more violence in my name right now." I cut a look at my friend. "How do you and Clay deal with the speculation that follows you the entire season?"

"Clay mostly ignores it. I get that ignoring people's opinions is a luxury not everyone has. Even so, he's had to build up the thick skin. But the alternative is worse."

She doesn't have to remind me of the bad place he was in a couple of years ago. Fortunately, she was there to help him.

"At least Miles has you in his corner now," she goes on. "Are you going to the all-star game?"

"If Miles goes, I'd love to. But it isn't something we've discussed—from my end, because I didn't want to jinx his chances, and he probably didn't want to put pressure on me."

The terrain gets steeper. I refuse to slow down, and my heart rate picks up as my hiking shoes dig into the dirt.

"Well, voting closes tomorrow. Announcements are only a few days away."

Nova slips on a loose twig. "Oops!"

I grab her arm to keep her upright. "Don't fall and break anything. I'd have to call one of the guys to carry you back."

"Clay would happily do it, but I don't want to give

him an excuse to mess with his knee again." She laughs.

"Why did you agree to go hiking with me? You hate winter hiking."

"But I love you." Her wide smile eases the tension in my chest.

"I love you too," I say and mean it. Nova's friendship is one of the greatest gifts I've found here in Denver.

We start back up, slower this time.

"You ever decide you don't want to do this art thing any longer, you could have a long and successful career as a motivational speaker," I inform her. "You and Clay could take your act on the road—high-performance stress management."

She laughs. "Can you imagine Clay being a motivational speaker?"

"He'd be great. Except for the motivational part. And the speaking part."

Nova's phone vibrates, and when she glances at it her eyes light up. "Yes! I have some interest in a show from this gallery in LA I've followed for years."

"That's amazing!" I peer over her shoulder at the profile for Coastal Gallery.

They have a large following and have featured an eyebrow-raising array of prominent artists. Working with them would be huge for my friend's career.

"There's a problem." She makes a face. "When I show them my new pieces, they find an excuse or ask about things I've done before this year."

There's a clearing in the trees, and I force myself up the last couple feet and step out into it. A drop-off in front of us offers a sweeping view of mountains and a frozen river.

Nova's right behind me. "Oh wow. It's gorgeous."

I turn toward my friend, soaking in her flushed cheeks, the pink braids sticking out from under her hat. She's such a bright spirit with a kind of earnest fearlessness that's admirable.

"It's like you said—change is hard," I decide. "But we'll show the world that the beauty is worth the risk, starting with Coastal Gallery."

3

MILES

For most of my life, I wasn't invested in who was the big or little spoon. Cuddling with another person, sharing their space, never made my wish list.

But since Brooke moved in, there's no hotel bed that can stack up to the feel of this woman in my arms. Her skin against mine. Her back fitted to my front so that I can see her, smell her, feel her. It's Brooke in surround sound.

She can call me out, wrap me around her damned finger, but she's still my little spoon.

I brush her hair back to murmur against her ear, "Morning, Princess."

She grumbles a response.

Without any intervention, she can sleep until

noon. Maybe that's why I was able to seduce her—through coffee. Whatever the reason, I'll take it.

Last night, I went over to Grams's new retirement home to check that the new furniture I got her had been delivered and installed. It also took my mind off the shoe deal. The first payment is supposed to come in once we announce all-star week, whether I land a spot or not.

But I haven't heard anything lately, and the meeting with Chloe and management is still on my mind.

Apologize to Kevin.

When I updated Brooke on the meeting yesterday, I left that part out.

There's no way I'm apologizing to the piece of shit who thought he could make her life hell—the one who seems as if he's decided he's not over the tiny bit of payback he got when I slammed my fist into his face years ago and told him never to go near her again.

My hand twinges thinking about it.

He's not coming back.

If he knows what's good for him in that preppy head, he won't be back.

I force myself to relax and skim her shoulder, down her arm, across her stomach where her top has ridden up. "Big day today."

Brooke's eyes fly open. "Grams."

She's awake and already trying to shift out of bed. I drag her back.

"What's wrong?" Brooke asks, turning to face me. "I mean, except for the all-star game and Grams and the shittiest blast from my past showing up at your work."

My hands lace behind her neck, playing with the hair at her nape.

Her lashes lower to half-mast, the light peeking through the curtains shining on her golden skin, and I remind myself how fucking lucky I am to be with her, touching her, existing in her damned orbit.

And that's why I don't say it. If I'm pissed off over it, I can only imagine how livid she'd be.

Because I've been waiting so fucking long for this girl, and now that I have her—sort of, almost, or so I tell myself since she sleeps in my bed, teaches my dog tricks, and carefully curates the metric ton of her designer shoes in my closet—I can't bring myself to toss those words on the pile of everything else burning in my life right now.

Everything bad is outside the walls of this room.

I grin. "Except for those? Nothing."

"DAMN. IS THAT AN ECHO?" I turn around in Grams's new living room, extending my arms. "This place is big enough you'll be hosting *Bridgerton* balls every weekend."

Grams laughs. "That's one way to make friends."

It's rewarding to see her smiling on move-in day because it's taken a ton of work to get here. Visiting different places, convincing her it was the right idea, going back and forth with my accountant to ensure there would be enough to cover everything she'd need today and always.

This retirement home is ten minutes farther away than the last one, but I'll sleep better knowing about the round-the-clock care and other safety features they reminded me of when I went in to sign the contracts.

"If you need help with your hair for these soirées, let me know. I've got a good hand with feathers." Brooke glances over from where she's arranging Grams's photos on a shelf.

"Feathers, huh?" I murmur near Brooke's ear.

She laughs, but I'm already making a mental note to order one of everything from Victoria's Secret.

"Well? What do you think?" I ask Grams as she walks around her new place.

Her smile has faded. Hopefully, it's just tiredness setting in after a busy day. She takes in the bedroom and bathroom, both decorated in her favorite colors and complete with plenty of handrails to help avoid falls like the one that had her in a cast for weeks.

At least the cast has finally come off.

"Where are my games?" Grams asks.

"I put them in the coffee table drawer." I motion that way.

"Oh."

Brooke looks between us. "If we slide this over here..." She rearranges immediately, retrieving Monopoly, plus Clue and Life, and carrying them to the shelf. "That way you can see them."

Relief softens Grams's features.

We finish organizing things before walking Grams down to dinner. It's not even five, but they eat early at these places.

"Don't charm them all at once," I warn. "Or people will start doing crazy things for one of those ball invites."

"I'll do my best." She laughs, her eyes getting damp at the corners. "I'm lucky to have such a kind grandson. I'm so proud of you, Miles. The boy you were and the man you've become."

Shit. She's going to make me cry too. After all she's done for me, no other accolade can measure up to knowing Grams admires and respects me.

"Yeah, well, I'll get the Kodiaks into playoffs and make you proud again."

"It's not only about basketball."

"Don't tell our owner that. Or the GM. Or my agent."

I hug her and help her find a seat with another woman who introduces herself immediately.

Two watchful staff are already there, helping residents and chatting with them.

My hand finds Brooke's as we head for the doors. Halfway there, I pull up. "Did we forget something? Her meds—"

"Her pill dispenser is in the bathroom on the counter. The staff have her list so they can check in with her." Brooke tugs me forward.

"Right." I shake my head.

Now that this moment is here, I'm reminded how many fewer adult decisions I've had to make than most people. Since college, every aspect of my health has been prescribed, my hours are filled with games and practice and treatment and travel.

The team's sports psychologists are always reminding us to control what we can.

This was something I could control.

I hope I did the right thing.

"It's going to be great," she promises as we step outside.

My thoughts shift to Brooke.

Emotions that are so big they threaten to take me out fill my chest, stretch my ribs.

It's not that they're new exactly. It's almost as if they've always taken up space in the dark closet of my mind, but I've been afraid to look at them for too long or I'll be found out. But since she moved in, I've found myself leaving the door open. I glance at them when I pass, even nod in acknowledgment.

Lately, they don't wait for me to come looking. They pop out and make themselves known at every damned interval.

Does she feel it too?

I don't want to put that kind of pressure on her, especially with everything going on.

One more thing I can control.

"Time to grab dinner?" she asks.

"Uh, yeah."

I shake off the overwhelming feelings and drive us downtown. On the way, I call my favorite restaurant to ask if they have a table for us. They confirm but ask if we can wait until six when they officially open.

Since we're not in a hurry, I find parking a few blocks away. On our way to the restaurant, we pass a park with a basketball court. Some teenagers are playing pickup, one even wearing shorts despite the cold and snow at the edge of the court. The asphalt is warm enough to be dry, and their sneakers fly across it.

I'm itching to join them.

It's barely a minute before one of the guys looks over and yanks on his friend's shirt. "Look. Is that...?"

"Shit, it is."

The game stops, and I wave. "Don't let me interrupt."

"Are you kidding? We all play on our high school teams." He names two local schools. "We watch every Kodiaks game on TV."

"You ever been to one?" I ask.

He shakes his head. "Not since last year. You seen how much resale tickets go for now?"

"Maybe if you keep losing," one of them says helpfully. Another smacks him lightly on the side of the head.

I make a mental note to get home game tickets sent to the teams of the two schools.

The main guy who's been speaking confers under his breath with a couple of others. "Hey, can we get a picture?"

Brooke nudges my shoulder. "We've got time for more than a picture."

I turn back to the teens. More than one of them is looking at her. I can't blame them, and they're young enough I'm not going to give them shit if she doesn't mind.

"You can have a picture on one condition: let me play."

Half a dozen sets of brows shoot up. "Hell yes."

I shrug out of my jacket and pass it to her. "Can you keep this for me?"

"Go get 'em." Brooke winks.

I pull her close for a hard kiss, ignoring the hollers that go up behind me. "Thanks," I say when I let her go.

I'm in jeans and a sweater, but my shoes are decent enough for jogging a few steps around a city court.

We play three-on-three, other guys rotating off to make room. I take it easy on the first play.

"That's all you got?" the main kid asks.

Then I school them a little. I dribble past them and cut to the basket. Then I steal the ball down the other end, taking it to the perimeter to hit a three.

They're eating it up.

It's fun to play with them. I show them a few moves.

When I glance over, Brooke's got her phone up.

I check my watch and realize we've been at this nearly half an hour. "Thanks for the game," I say, and they groan in protest as I lift a hand. "Good luck with your season."

"Wait. Give me your handle," Brooke says to the main guy.

"Are you asking him out?" one of the others asks as he provides it, and snorts erupt amongst the teens.

"Nice try," Brooke says dryly without looking up. "There. The video's all yours."

They're still giddy when I put my jacket back on and we start for the restaurant, my heart thudding a little more and the blood thrumming in my veins.

"It was cool of you to send them that video," I say as we head up the sidewalk side by side, her taking two steps for every one of mine.

Brooke laughs. "They'll keep it forever. But first, they're going to post it, and it will spread like wildfire. Your shoe company will see it. So will Kodiaks management, which will remind them they made the right choice."

My mouth works for a second. "But... how do you know it'll spread?"

She smiles. "Trust me."

The walk sign comes up, and we start across the street.

I shake my head. "You're scary good sometimes, you know that?"

"I know," she says evenly. "You afraid of me?"

I pull her against my side, wondering if she can feel my heart skip. "Never." Guilt kicks in my gut at what I'm still keeping from her. "There's something I need to tell you."

We make it to the other sidewalk and pass a few groups of pedestrians before I speak again.

"Chloe wants me to apologize to Kevin."

She blinks. "What?"

"In public," I confirm.

Princess and I are a lot of things, but quiet isn't one of them. Now, silence stretches between us.

"She's right," she says at last.

It's my turn to be caught off guard. I pull up, unsure I've heard her right. "I'm not going through with it."

She stops too, lifting her chin. "You should. There's no getting out of it. He has nothing at stake here."

I think of the photos I have saved. "Wouldn't say that—"

"I mean right now," she presses. "Think about what's on the line for you."

"He's here for you, not for me." The words are out before I think about how they'd sound.

Her eyes widen. "You're right. This is my fault."

I pull her close to my side and curse myself for saying it. "That's not what I meant, Princess."

But the rest of the night, I'm thinking about it, and I know she is too.

4

BROOKE

The video goes viral.

Millions of views and a ton of shares mean it's a slam dunk that the shoe sponsor has seen it.

It doesn't hurt that Miles looks fantastic in the video.

Sure, a few hundred of the views might be mine, justifiably ogling my boyfriend.

My gaze drags to a comment near the bottom of the post.

No one's that good.

Garrett sure as hell isn't.

A dozen upvotes isn't many given the hundred plus comments. Still, I click on the two replies.

After the fight with Kevin and the team's press release, it felt as if the worst had blown over.

Miles needs this shoe deal for his grandmother. More than that, he deserves it. He's worked so damn hard this season, and for years before that. He's always shown up and been a team player.

My mom's words come back about things only heating up from here. She's suspicious by nature and necessity. It's her job to scan the environment for any possible problem.

It's not my nature anymore though.

"See something you like?" Chloe's voice pulls me out of my daydream.

I lower the phone. "Always." I hold out the flowers I bought.

"What are these, a bribe?" She turns the vase in her hands, admiring it.

"They're a thank-you. For having Miles's back with James and Harlan."

She motions me inside. Her office is large with a window that looks out toward the mountains. She's got a few years on me, but she's already head of PR with several staff. All the time I spent chasing after Elise, I'm not sure I fully appreciated what Chloe's accomplished.

"Want a drink?" Chloe shuts the door after me, then reaches into the mini fridge behind her desk.

"I should probably turn down alcohol."

"Just as well because I have water and Powerade."

She shifts back to reveal a fridge full of rows of colored drinks.

"Wow. Every flavor?"

"Sponsorship deals."

"I'm good with water."

She pulls out and sets one in front of me with a glass.

"So, the team has some work to do."

"It's been a tough season. Sponsors and fans see you win once, they expect it to happen again. But it takes luck and skill."

"Is that the excuse the team uses when they lose?"

"No. It buys us time to figure out how to win." Her eyes glint. "You must be here to talk about the job."

"If the offer still stands."

Chloe nods.

"Great." I take a breath. "Can you tell me more about the day-to-day?"

I ignore the glass and twist off the lid of the bottle as Chloe walks through the basics—liaising with the social media lead to grow brand presence, looking for ways to improve the team's visibility and reputation.

Being an influencer is what I know, but this could

be a way for me to build on those skills in a different way.

"It's long hours but limited travel. I often go to away games with the team, but with rare exceptions, you'd be based here," she confirms.

That all sounds doable. But I have a question.

"Why me?"

"With anyone else, I'd be worried about you coming in with rose-colored glasses. You understand enough about both PR and the team to know it's not always sexy and no job is perfect. But this one is a fantastic position to build your skills and resume, and there are chances to advance."

On paper, it's a great opportunity. The salary she mentioned would be more than enough to pay my expenses.

Still, I'm hesitating, though I can't put my finger on why.

"I need a few more days. Just with everything going on."

Chloe's brows lift. "Okay."

"I actually need a favor. Miles's apology for the incident with Kevin—any way he can get out of it? Public service?"

She shakes her head. "No way. If he dodges this, it'll piss off management."

The image of the Kodiaks' owner appears in my head. "But it wasn't Miles's fault."

"I know. We all eat shit for things that aren't our fault every day," Chloe reminds me. "If you want to help, you could try to keep him out of trouble for the rest of the season."

"I was trying," I mutter.

"You want to do something more active?" she asks dryly. "Like a guerilla campaign filming him playing with a bunch of kids at a city court?"

I inspect my nails innocently. "You saw that."

"Me and a couple million others. James included. The video was smart but risky."

The team's been playing better this week. They've won two and dropped one, but every game matters more as we hit the trade deadline. Teams are down to the wire now. It's organizations' last chance to make major moves before committing for the rest of the year.

"James and Harlan running around with any last-minute trades?" I ask.

"That I couldn't talk about." She tilts her head. "Now if you were a member of the organization..." Her long fingers twist her badge in the air. "You'd get the inside track on everything. Plus, free lunch every day. I could score you an office."

It does sound really appealing. With the Vivaro

problems, my brand partnerships have dried up. Working for the Kodiaks would give me a security I haven't had.

I scan the office, taking in the official brochures and photos and awards tacked up on the walls. "I don't believe you."

Chloe frowns. "About the perks?"

"No, the all-star announcement. You have to prepare to reveal it to the players, the family. As much as they want us to believe it's all a surprise, it can't be. Blink once for yes, twice for no." I lean in.

She snorts, clearly impressed by my tenacity. "If he does get in, he had more help than yours and mine." She folds her arms. "Jay had Miles's back every bit as much."

Surprise sets me on my heels. "Jay didn't say anything to me."

"He's softening... or his disgust for your ex is worse than his feud with Miles."

Her tone is matter of fact, but there's kindness in it too. She loves this team.

This woman is only a few years older than me, but she's the kind of person I always pictured being. Cool, fun, accomplished. Not the too perfect of the Kappas, never a toe out of line, but real.

I could do far worse than working for her.

"Why did you and my brother break up?" I hear

myself ask. "I know you were serious once. He never talked about anyone else. He hasn't been the same since."

Something flickers through her dark eyes. It takes a lot to catch Chloe off-guard, and I've never seen a reporter do it. Now, though, she looks vulnerable.

"That's another thing I can't talk about," she says at last.

"Unless I take the job?" I supply.

"*Especially* if you take the job," she says wryly, recovering.

Her office phone rings. Whatever number is on the call display has her grabbing for it.

"Yes, I can speak to the commissioner's office." Her eyes flash a warning for me to be quiet.

Anticipation burns me from the inside out. It takes everything in me not to hit the speakerphone button. Still, I'm straining to hear what's said over the phone.

I don't catch a damn word.

"Understood. Thank you." She clicks off.

"Well?!" I demand.

"Time to get back to work." Chloe rises and drinks the rest of her water in a long gulp. "Not every team gets a player in the all-star game."

My eyes shut as disappointment floods me.

Miles isn't going. All this work was for nothing.

I hear a ping and blink. The empty water bottle hits the bottom of the recycling bin without bouncing off the sides.

Chloe's squared up toward the bin. She lowers her hands slowly, gaze still fixed on the makeshift basket as her lips curve with satisfaction.

"Some teams get two."

MILES

"You're making *me* coffee this morning?" I pad into the kitchen in sweats and a hoodie, my hair still wet from the shower.

"Can't let you steal all the glory." Brooke holds out a mug then goes to make one for herself.

I lean against the counter and take an appreciative sip.

This morning, she got dressed before me, in jeans that hug her curves and a soft cream-colored sweater. Her face is fresh, her bronze skin glowing with a hint of makeup that makes her eyes look even bigger and her lips fuller.

"This is really better than joining me in the

shower?" I say, my voice full of doubt as I remember the offer she turned down.

"Needed the caffeine stimulation."

"The shower would've been plenty stimulating." I set down the mug and step closer.

She has this habit of pulling her hair back in a curly ponytail before she gets ready in the morning, but today, it's already smooth.

It's a tipoff.

Brooke never gets ready without a purpose, and now, I'm using every ounce of my brain to try and figure out what it was today.

"Mmm. As tempting as the offer was, it would've made us late," she murmurs.

"Fuck the calendar. You can't be late for life, Princess." I pull her against me, my lips brushing along her jawline.

Right now, Brooke's the best part of mine.

"You weren't always this sappy," she accuses.

If she only knew what's going through my head right now.

"Sweet," I correct. "I just hide it in front of the guys."

She rolls her eyes. "Fine. But don't go spouting poetry on the way to the grocery store."

"I'll save the iambic pentameter for dinners out." I grin, and she can't resist either.

Just like I can't resist kissing her again.

She's been distracted the past day. Probably since our disagreement over apologizing to Kevin.

I hate it when we're not on the same page.

She rests her hands on my chest before pushing me back. "Focus," she commands.

I groan, because her telling me what to do is one of the things that turns me on most about her.

"You're getting good at this," I comment as she finally turns back to the espresso machine. It's sexy as hell to watch her make coffee.

Now, I'm picturing her hands on me instead, capable, insistent.

Fuck it. We have time.

I can make her come at least twice, which is the minimum, even for a quickie.

Got to keep my standards up.

"Don't get used to it."

I pounce on her words. "Aha! So, it *is* a special occasion. You're going to have to tell me before I leave for practice."

"I'll come with you."

I do a double take, my suspicion dialing up another ten notches.

She turns away, but I grab her by the waist, my hands finding the soft skin under her sweater.

"Brooke Ellis, you know something."

She ducks out of my grip and grabs a mug out of the cupboard, doing a little shimmy on the way.

"Thought you were meeting Chloe about the job."

"I did. I told her I needed to think it over."

I was trying my best to be a supportive boyfriend; as much as I'd love for her to take it so I'd get to see her at the office, it might mean she'd have a more demanding schedule that would eat into our time together.

Plus, there was the issue of her wanting to be independent. She had wanted distance from her brother's basketball life, and now she was dating one of his teammates. Setting up an office at the Kodiaks could make it even harder for her.

"That's all you talked about?" I grab her legs and lift her in the air. She screeches and drops the mug, eliciting a little yip from Waffles, who's watching from the dining room.

"You broke a mug." Her legs go around my hips.

"No way. You knew?!" I'm not talking about the mug.

"You're going to step on it and hurt yourself." She still is.

I don't know whether her mouth finds mine first or the other way around. It doesn't matter because I can't do anything that's not kissing her.

I've been to the all-star weekend, but only for the three-point competition.

Getting named to the actual team means you're legit. Out of the hundreds of guys in the league, you're one of a couple dozen that coaches and reporters and fans agree is the best of the best.

I've always settled for good enough. Being part of a group, not standing out.

I'm laughing when I pull my mouth from hers. "The data crunchers fucked up and picked my number by accident."

She arches a brow. "Oh, wait, you're not the Miles Garrett who's been putting up twenty-five points a night on his shorthanded team? The one who's been logging extra hours in the gym and watching tape, who stepped up the past few months in a way no one saw coming but they all should have?"

Damn. Her words touch a part of me that I didn't know needed to be touched. The way she sees me makes me want to be even better—for her, my team, myself.

Brooke cups my face as her dark eyes go serious. "Well, then, just tell them they've got the wrong guy and you're not interested."

"Let's not rush into anything. I am pretty great, actually."

"Really?"

"Mhmm."

"At what?"

I toss her over my shoulder and start for the hall.

"Miles!" Brooke screeches, though it's closer to a bellow—probably thanks to the angle and where my shoulder's pressing into her stomach. "We're going to be late!"

"Too bad. Going to show you exactly what I'm good at before we leave."

WE MAKE it to the car twenty minutes behind.

But my girl is three orgasms ahead, so that's good math.

The entire drive over, I'm buzzing, and it's not from the coffee. I crank the music, whistling along the entire time.

I'm excited for the day, grateful to have her at my side. Nothing could ruin this moment.

"I need you to do something for me," Brooke says as we pull into the parking lot at the stadium.

"Anything, Princess." I shift out of the car and open the back to grab my gear bag.

She appears next to me. "Apologize for the fight with Kevin."

Slamming the hatchback isn't an option, so I stab the power close button. "Anything except that."

I'd started to think the disagreement had passed, that she was going to accept my decision and move on.

I shoulder my bag and start for the door, frustration edging into my anticipation. Security holds the door, nodding to me. I nod back.

Brooke catches up partway down the hall. We pass a camera crew that's got a sports network's name on it.

"I talked to Chloe," Brooke says at my side. "It's important."

Her heels click along, taking two strides for every one of mine.

"And what will they do?" I shove a hand through my hair and slow down a bit. "We stalled—thanks to you—and it'll blow over."

"It's not over," she says with certainty. "They could fine you, trade you—fire you."

Her words make me pull up.

She's standing in the middle of the hall, breathing heavily. I drop the bag at my side and close the distance between us. I take her arms in my hands.

"You're the one who stands up for what's right," I

remind her, my gut knotting tightly. "Who tells the bad guys to fuck off, usually in public."

She looks past me, brows drawn. "This affects other people. Your team needs you. Your grand-mother needs you."

My throat tightens. Brooke's not wrong, and the reminder makes it all hurt more.

I have pride, but more than that, I'm not about to lie down in front of a piece of shit who treated her like she was worse than replaceable—who used her and lied to her, then dared to act like she was his property when she never was.

Not when they were dating, and sure as hell not now.

"You want me to do it for them?"

A nod.

"And if I don't?"

"Then do it for me." Her eyes shine.

The trouble I caught him in, the pact we made, plays back in my mind. I don't owe him anything. Back then, he tried to hurt Brooke—succeeded, come to that—and all he got from it was a black eye.

Brooke doesn't move, almost as if she knows what's going through my mind.

"Princess," I say under my breath. "You're the reason I can't."

I turn and head for the locker room, smacking my fist into the wall on the way.

We're running hard drills, sweat sticking my jersey to my back, when Coach calls for a break.

I've tossed back half a Powerade when Atlas shoves my shoulder and nods behind me.

James and Harlan are standing at the edge of the court, Chloe at their side.

Is he here to tell me to apologize too?

I don't realize I've said it out loud until Clay grunts at my side.

"No love lost between me and that man, but what did happen with that fight last week?"

I debate how much to say. "Back in college, I roughed up Kevin pretty bad. He deserved it for the way he treated Brooke."

"You get in shit for it?"

I shake my head. "Nah, because I got photos of him. He wanted to know if I still had them."

He blinks. "And you said...?"

"I said, who the fuck knows what I have stored away?"

Clay grabs a towel and scrubs it across his face

and the tattoos covering his shoulders and arms. "Why does he have a problem with you now?"

"Probably doesn't like seeing me with the woman he thought was his. If he has an ounce of brain in his douchebag head, he realizes what he let get away."

"I get it, but we need this. Sometimes the biggest plays you make happen off the court."

James finally steps forward.

"In a moment, we're going to turn on the broadcast. The all-star committee is going to announce their next selections: Miles Garrett from the Denver Kodiaks."

A roar goes up from the guys that rivals anything from a full stadium.

My grin splits my face.

"And Clayton Wade will be repeating for his fifth performance? Sixth? Who the hell knows how many," Harlan says with a grin, and the guys laugh.

I turn to Clay and clap him on the back in congratulations.

"You deserve it, man," I laugh.

"You do too."

But it's the words Clay says before I release him that stick with me long after practice.

GARRETT ISSUES STATEMENT ON EVE OF
ALL-STAR GAME:

"Fighting is not the answer, but I will always stand
up for the people I care about."

5

─────

BROOKE

Jay: Give Hawkins a message: we're coming for Boston after all-star break

Damon: Sign it with a kiss

Miles: Should the kiss be from me or Clay?

Atlas: Both

Damon: You better check with the girls first

Brooke: Nova and I approve this use of lips

"I never thought this would end with us on opposite sides," I say as I fold my arms.

Nova blinks up at me with eyes rimmed

with glittery gold liner. "It doesn't have to be that way."

In a cream outfit with gold boots, her hair in expert waves for TV, she could be some kind of WAG fairy.

"Oh, I think it does. You see this name?" I call over the murmur of the capacity Vegas crowd, pointing at the back of my jersey. "That's my loyalty tonight."

The all-star jerseys are blue for the Western Conference and gold for the East. It's nearly impossible to get them ahead of the game, but I used my contacts to not only score one but have it altered into a shift dress that shows off my legs.

Underneath, I'm wearing over-the-knee dark-blue suede boots. My hair is smoothed back in a glossy high ponytail.

I arch a brow and inspect my manicure—not Kodiaks' purple but blue, part of the outfit I've been putting together all week.

Nova leans in. "Too bad we're besties and I know all your secrets, Brooke Ellis."

I can't help grinning in response.

Tonight, Miles and Clay are on opposite sides.

Nova, Chloe, Mari, and I are all here to cheer on Miles and Clay. But the battle lines have been redrawn tonight, with players from the same regular season team split up based on the captains' picks.

"You'd better, because you really don't want to make her your enemy." We both turn to see Jay make his way into the seats at the end with Rookie.

Surprise nearly has me dropping my beer. I didn't figure my brother would come, but maybe he did it out of solidarity with his teammates.

"She holds a grudge. This one time when I was fourteen and she was twelve, she wanted to come to an event with me, and I said no. She was still in that tagalong phase. She snuck out and followed me anyway, made friends with the organizers, and got in on her own. Little sis had a crush on one of the players."

"That was over in a second. His twin had the most amazing hair, and I needed to ask her how she did it," I counter.

His lips twitch. Not quite a smile, but I'm secretly pleased to see it anyway.

Jay's gaze falls to my jersey, but if it bothers him to see me wearing something with Miles's name on it, he doesn't comment on it.

Progress, I decide.

"In that case"—Nova holds out a hand to me—"may the best all-star win."

On the court, the players are announced one at a

time. The crowd erupts with each new name. One player after another steps out onto the court to acknowledge the applause and give the cameramen time for a closeup for the millions watching on TV.

I clap for Clay when he rises and waves to the crowd. I'm not a total monster.

But when they say Miles's name, I scream my lungs out.

He looks fantastic in the all-star uniform as he steps onto the court, his dark hair falling over his face. I told him it was getting long and to cut it before the game, but he said he needed the luck.

Nova hollers as loudly for Miles as she does for her husband.

Miles's gaze finds mine, and his grin widens.

Damn, he's hot.

I've never been that affected by basketball players, but this one is the exception. Turns out all the banter and teasing for the past few years made for wicked foreplay.

I think back to our conversation before the game.

"What do I get if I win?" Miles asked.

"A massage."

"With what?" Dark eyebrows wiggled.

I laughed, but before I could relax too much, he came right back at me.

"Tell you what, Princess. We win tonight, I want you

on my cock the second we get back to the hotel room. Until you can't feel anything but me, everywhere. Until you can't remember what it's like without me inside you. Until the only name you know is mine."

"What about my name?"

"Don't worry. I'll be saying it enough for both of us."

"That statement he issued is causing a lot of ripples." Jay's voice brings me back.

The words issued by Miles's agent replay in my mind. They're burned behind my eyes. Since the moment I read them, I've been holding my breath.

"I told him to apologize."

"We both know that was hardly an apology."

Nova leans over. "You're supposed to cheer equally for both your teammates," she says to Jay.

"I'm here, aren't I? Besides, can't cheer too loud. Hawkins is on the same team." Jay straightens in his seat, frowning.

The energy is off the wall for tip-off.

Clay's starting on one end, Miles on the other.

The atmosphere on the court should be lighter than a real game because they're playing for charity. But it's an exhibition of the best basketball talent on the planet and the players who eat, sleep, and breathe competition. The guys on the floor are the gods of basketball, and the crowd has come to worship.

The first couple of plays are each team feeling out themselves and the other side.

Each time the ball goes in and the other team jogs back, there are some jokes and light trash talking on the floor. We can't hear what's said from here, but we can witness the exchanges.

Miles gets his first shot attempt and misses. I groan.

A few plays later, the ball finds him in the corner. Another miss.

The coach for the evening sits him on the bench.

It's not just Miles. The West team is a step slow out of the gate, already behind by six.

"Miles and Hawkins are going down," Jay observes. "The East is locked in."

"Care to make a little wager?" I turn toward him, folding my arms.

"How much?" Jay asks.

"Five hundred?"

"That's a lot for you to lose."

"I'm not going to lose." I nod to Miles, doing a fist pump. *Let's go*, I mouth.

The next time they put him in, he locks it down. One of his teammates finds him near half court, and he takes it all the way down into the key for a dunk.

I'm out of my seat hollering. He must hear me,

because his gaze finds me as he's running back on defense. I turn to show Miles the back of my jersey.

He flashes a heated grin in my direction.

Miles's team gets up by halftime.

"If you Venmo me tonight, I might even buy you a drink at the club later," I inform my brother.

"Can I have one?" Nova asks.

"You're my friend. You can have two," I say generously.

At halftime, Rookie and Jay float around the crowd to talk to other players and friends from the league who are watching. Nova and I grab food. On the way back, I find myself in my seat next to Jay.

"Where's Rookie?" I ask.

"Bathroom. Nova?"

"Same." I nod.

We're quiet a minute.

"Popcorn?" He holds it out.

"Only if there are M&Ms in it."

"Obviously."

It's a peace offering. I reach in and pop a few pieces of popcorn and candy into my mouth. The sweet and salty flavors collide on my tongue. It reminds me of summer nights in high school, watching movies with friends or tagging along to my brother's games.

"I like these nights," I say. They're a reminder of what's fun in the league.

"They don't change anything. It's for the fans, the owners, the guys who make money. Next week, we're back in the gym and playing for the same stakes we've been going after all year."

"That's what makes this matter more," I decide.

As the game resumes in the second half, the crowd flows back into their seats. On the far side behind the bench, I catch sight of a man who makes me do a double take. But the moment I think I've seen him, he's gone.

The game resumes, and once again, we're focused on the court.

By the time the final whistle blows and the confetti descends from the rafters—Miles's team wins by five, and the crowd goes crazy—I've nearly convinced myself it was just my imagination.

6

MILES

You've never partied if you've never been out after a Vegas all-star game.

Dozens of clubs and bars on the Strip are ready to welcome fans and players, and we have an invite to the best of the best.

ICE nightclub, owned by Harrison King, is the place to be this year. His wife is one of the biggest producers and DJs in the world, but despite their public personas, they've managed to keep the story of how their relationship started mostly private.

Brooke, Clay, Nova, and I have barely gotten inside ICE when a woman cuts through the crowd to us. She's about our age with strong features and dark hair. At first, I wonder if she's a hostess—she's definitely beautiful enough—but she's too familiar and too relaxed for that. Nova holds her arms wide to the woman, who lets herself be drawn into a light hug.

"Didn't see your name on the marquee," Brooke calls over the music.

Raegan Madani, whom I recognize now that she's up close, mouths something that looks as if it includes the word "vacation." Her mouth curves, a tiny lift at one corner that barely registers in the darkness.

Brooke introduces me, and Raegan throws me a half nod. Her attention, even for a second, isn't careless. Her gaze is the kind of intense that makes you feel as if she sees everything you've ever been or wanted to be.

"Well played, gentlemen." The man who sweeps in wearing a dark suit has a British accent that's obvious even over the pulsing beat. His hair is light. Everything else about him dark.

Clay and I shake Harrison's hand in greeting. He's giving Daniel Craig-era Bond even before he shifts an arm around Raegan's shoulders, her fingers lacing casually through his. Brooke's gaze flicks up and down him.

"You better be eyeing the suit," I murmur in her ear.

She laughs, eyes warming with appreciation. "You worried?"

"Nah. I know exactly how to make you scream my name."

Brooke looks next level tonight in a sparkly silver dress and heels. I like her hair every way, but tonight, she's straightened it so that it falls down her back in a curtain.

I want to soak up every moment of this experience, but I also want to drag Brooke somewhere private and show her exactly how much it means to me that she's here.

"Harry and Rae"—as Harrison insists we call them—show us to the best VIP booth in the place and inform us that each of the six booths by the dance floor have been reserved for players and guests. Ours is the most private, but each booth has black leather seats tall enough to shield all but the tallest VIPs.

Over the back of our booth, I spot other players from the game, including Hawkins in the next booth over with a couple other players and a few vaguely familiar faces—a couple of actors, I think, and a musician.

Our first round goes down fast. It's a celebration, and after the long day of activity, I can feel the alcohol in my system.

Harry doesn't linger, but Rae stays for a drink, chatting with Nova and Brooke.

"To your first of many games." Clay holds up his glass.

The guy doesn't drink alcohol during the season. For a moment, I imagine doing the same, but the next drink washes away any reluctance.

"Where did Jay and Chloe go?" Nova calls.

Brooke shrugs.

We're distracted when Rookie and Atlas come by the booth for a round. One song blends into another. The vibe is practically giddy—we're young and rich and have a week off, so what the fuck is there not to love?

I grab Brooke. "Dance with me."

She tilts her head. "Are you any good?"

I grin. "I'm an all-star, baby."

Brooke's eyes roll, but she lets me tug her onto the floor.

I've got moves, but the second we're out there, it's all about her. She's unselfconscious, moving to the music, both hands in the air. Her curvy hips sway, the shimmery fabric of the dress clinging to her body.

She lifts the phone in the air and snaps a sexy pic. Then changes the angle so it's just our faces and texts both to me.

"What's that one for?" I tease her.

"Grams! Figured she could do with less side boob and more of you." She winks.

I love you.

I've never said that to a woman, but the words are there, not even waiting for me to come looking for them. They're in the living room of my mind, in the foyer, busting out the front door and parading down the street with a ten-piece band.

I love Grams. I love basketball. I love Waffles because he loves me so much it's impossible not to reciprocate. I love my friends, but in that collective way where if one of them drifted away, I'd find others and it would be cool.

Loving Brooke is another thing entirely.

Doing it from a distance was safer. I could care all I wanted when she was in school and I got drafted. Then later, when she was hanging out with someone else, or I was—when she was my best friend's little sister and I was the guy who looked out for her because it was the right thing to do.

I can't go back to loving her from across the room. I won't be able to watch her in the stands or play laser tag against her or ask what she's planning for Jay's birthday party and not know she's mine.

But when I pull back to open my mouth, she's looking past my shoulder.

"What's wrong?" I ask over the music.

She smiles quickly. "Nothing." But she can't hide the fact that her head's somewhere else.

It hurts a little.

"Garrett, man." Another player cuts in to say hi. "The hell was that in the media?" he laughs.

"An apology."

He exchanges a look with Brooke. "Didn't look like one."

He excuses himself to make conversation with another group of players.

"That what you think too?" I ask Brooke. After a couple of drinks, I'm not subtle.

"Honestly?"

"Always."

"Your statement was possibly worse than saying nothing," she decides. "It could piss off James and Harlan. Not like I don't like to see them work for their money."

I'm a chill guy, but all year I've been digging deep and find more of myself. More to give the team, the world. Feels as if I've been excavated with a metal shovel digging down through rock. You go that deep with a tool that sharp, you're going to leave some rough edges.

"Another round," I say when we get back to the booth. "Order for me and I'll be right back?"

Brooke nods and settles in, but I head to the back hallway toward the bathrooms. Inside, I bump into Hawkins.

"Nice game tonight," he says.

"Team effort, man. You played all right yourself."

"Once in a lifetime. Enjoy it," he says.

"First, you mean," I correct.

"No, I don't." He grins and I wait him out. "You're not Jordan or Kobe or Clay Wade. You're a diversion. Once you're done being amusing, they'll be on to the next guy who pulls his head out of his ass to build a streak for a few games. So will your girl. I've definitely seen her around all-star weekend a time or two."

He brushes past me before I can respond. My hands fist at my sides as I start to lurch after him, but I bump into the sink.

Trash talk is nothing new. I just didn't expect it from the guy I won a game with a few hours ago.

I know better than to let him under my skin. It's none of my fucking business what Brooke did or didn't do, but that doesn't mean it's not turning like a screw in my brain right now.

The door swings open, and in walks a group of young guys.

"Hey, Garrett, right? You're legendary." The guy who brushed in the door last is nearly my height but probably a college player from his age.

"Appreciate it," I manage. Even my mouth feels a step slow.

"Anytime. Your pranks are infamous. What you did with the rubber chicken a few years ago…" He cackles and continues past me, shaking his head.

What if Hawkins is right?

When I get back to the booth, I slide in next to Brooke. My arm brushes her bare shoulder as I reach for the bottle in the middle of the table.

Empty.

I order another round as our server clears the empty bottle.

Brooke tilts her head. "Are you okay?"

"Epic. Legendary," I go on with relish.

"Just one for him," Brooke calls to our server with a frown.

She leans her chin on a hand—a hand with brightly colored nails that blur. "If I knew I was going to carry you out of here, I'd have worn flats."

"Not going to happen. I'll carry you, Princess," I correct over the music after the woman leaves, nudging Brooke's leg with mine.

Over the back of the booth, I spot Hawkins with two women. One's pressing herself to his front, the other to his back.

I'm remembering what he said about Brooke. I try not to think about her hooking up with other guys here.

"How does this all-star weekend stack up to the

others?" I ask her before I can stop myself. "Because I know you used to come."

Her gaze is searching. "This one's pretty damn good. I'm here with you."

She means it. On some level, I feel her earnestness.

But that level is buried beneath too much alcohol and a raging insecurity that somehow reared its head in the last hour.

Between the bodies pressed together on the dance floor and the ones in the booths, I can't kick what Hawkins said.

"You were looking for something earlier," I say.

"I thought I saw someone familiar."

Someone she would've been with tonight if it wasn't for me?

The waitress brings a fresh drink, and I tip it back.

"Don't let me get in your way," I say with a grin as I set the empty glass on the table. It sticks to the surface.

Brooke shifts to face me more fully. Her bare knees brush my thigh, the shiny dress shifting further up her toned legs.

My chest is on fire. My fingers are tingling, and my head feels like cotton.

The expression on her face is all wrong, but I

can't place it before she motions me closer with a finger. I lift a brow, or try—my face is going numb—and lean in until my nose bumps hers.

"Garrett," Brooke says in my ear. "I'm here with you, okay? Don't make me question it."

I'm already buzzing, but I look over at Hawkins. He's laughing at me.

The next second, I'm out of the booth. I grab the front of his shirt. Warnings from my friend drift into my fuzzy ears.

I want to hit him.

The floor hits me first.

7

____

BROOKE

Heels were not made for keeping up with a gurney.

But, there's no way I'm leaving Miles as he bumps across the pavement between two paramedics from the ambulance to the hospital.

"He said he was feeling fine," I call as I follow, one hand on the cold side rail because I'm afraid if I put it on his shoulder, I'll lose my grip.

"You said he had several drinks?" One paramedic, a tall woman with a level voice, asks.

"More than usual," I admit.

The ambulance techs continue into the ER, and a nurse meets them there. She directs the gurney into a private room. I try not to think about the people in the waiting room who have to wait longer now that a basketball VIP is in the building.

"Wait here," one says as I try to head inside the room too.

I pace the halls, getting in the way more than once. I'm trying to wrap my head around what happened, but it's blurring together given the couple of drinks I had myself.

Miles was in a great mood when we went out, and he had every reason to be. Sure, there was some tension between him and the team this week, but nothing they couldn't set aside for a night like this.

But something changed at the club.

My phone rings—Nova.

"Where are you?" she demands.

Forty minutes later, she arrives along with Clay and my brother.

The earlier excitement in my friend's eyes has been replaced with worry.

I fill them in. "I don't know what happened. He wasn't acting like himself."

Nova nods. Gold glitter has started to flake onto her cheeks. "The all-star game is a weird night. He's been under a lot of pressure."

I instantly reject her assumption, which probably shows on my face. I can hide what I'm thinking but not in front of my best friend, not after the night we've had.

The halls are lined with people in all sorts of

dress. I suppose that's a Vegas thing. A kid with blond hair walks by, and I track him with my gaze.

"Excuse me. Did you come in with Mr. Garrett?" a doctor asks, consulting his clipboard.

"We all did," Jay says from across the room, but I'm there first.

"That's right."

His gaze flicks down my body, then intently zeroes in on my face. "We're still waiting for labs to come back. You said you were drinking. Anything else?"

"Like what?"

"Did Mr. Garrett ingest any other substances today or this evening?"

I cut a look back at my brother and Clay, who look every bit as surprised as I feel. "No."

The doctor studies me a moment longer as if I might change my mind but finally nods. "Do you know if he left any of his drinks unsupervised?"

"You think he was drugged." My mind is spinning.

The doctor shakes his head. "Without labs, I can't say for sure. But you can go in and see him. He's conscious but not at full alertness."

I don't wait for him to tell me twice.

Miles is in the hospital bed, his feet sticking over

the edge and his face unusually pale. I lean over the side, grabbing his hand in two of mine.

"Miles."

His eyes crack when I say his name. "Hey, Princess," he croaks. "What happened? I feel terrible."

I absently stroke his palm with my thumb.

"You don't remember?"

His head moves back and forth but barely, as if the effort costs him.

Did Mr. Garrett ingest any other substances?

I clear my throat. "You passed out. One moment you were talking to Hawkins, the next, you collapsed. The doctors are still running tests, but they're wondering if it wasn't only the alcohol."

His eyes close, from fatigue or because he's thinking it over. "Anyone notice?"

"Probably not," I lie. "Everyone had their own thing going on."

There was more than one phone out as the paramedics came in, but I don't want him worrying about that right now.

"But," I continue, "Jay's outside. Clay too. They want to make sure you're okay."

Miles nods and clears his throat. "Fuck, I'm thirsty. Is there any—"

"I'll get you a drink. Don't go anywhere."

His hand grabs my arm, but his grip is weak. "If you're going to take care of me, can you wait until I'm sure I'll remember it?"

"Absolutely not," I say, then brush my lips over his and straighten. I go to the nursing station outside the room. "Water?"

They go to fetch some.

"How is he?" Clay asks.

"What the hell happened?" Jay choruses.

I shake my head. "They think..." I swallow and look around to ensure no one can overhear. "They think he was drugged."

"That he was drugged or that he *took* drugs?"

My brother speaks with a tired urgency I don't recognize.

"The first. Obviously," I say, though I can't remember exactly what they said.

They exchange a look. "Let's go in and see him."

I watch them head in to see their friend and teammate before pressing a hand against my face.

Fuck.

I should have known something was wrong with him earlier.

Miles was having too much fun to realize. If only I'd noticed...

Being with him, I enjoyed not having to watch

myself. Miles himself told me he likes me when I let my guard down.

But this was a reminder that even if Miles wasn't going to judge me or hurt me, there were still forces out there in the world that could hurt us.

Nova approaches with her phone. "Harrison wants to know if Miles is okay."

"Tell him..." I search my mind for an answer that will put his mind at ease and is more or less true. "It was probably too much to drink after a busy day."

My friend types and hits Send. "Harrison says he's sending a limo and booked a private suite for him to recover, plus medical staff to keep an eye on him for the next forty-eight hours."

Gratitude fills me.

I accept the water from the nurse and run it back into Miles. He's already sleeping, so I set it on the table next to him before returning to my friend to watch through the doorway.

Nova steps closer.

"I'm sorry." Her whisper makes me hiccup a shaky breath.

"Thanks." I lean my head on her shoulder.

I'm tough. Still, it's one thing to deal with problems yourself and another to watch someone you care about go through them.

"Miles wouldn't take drugs. Everyone knows

that." Nova's voice has a strange lift to it, as though it's a question and not a statement.

My chest tightens as staff and equipment continue to fly past us.

"Everyone knows it," I echo.

8

MILES

**HOOPSNEWS UPDATE: GARRETT RELEASED
FROM HOSPITAL AFTER ALL-STAR GAME
AMIDST RUMORED DRUG USE**

"I promise I'm not lying in a ditch, Grams," I insist over the phone. "I'm fine. Good as new."

"But HoopsNews said—"

"Don't listen to that crap. I'll come visit tonight. We'll play Monopoly and you can finally sell me Indiana Avenue."

She chuckles, and for a moment, it's as if she's here at the practice facility with me. "I'm grateful Brooke was with you."

My chest twinges. "Me too."

I'm thinking back to that night. Too much of it is hazy, and my regret deepens.

"Miles. Doctor's here to see you," one of the trainers says from the doorway of the locker room.

"I heard that," Grams says over the line.

"Abundance of caution and all that. I'm healthy as ever. Promise." I say goodbye and click off.

I go to review my reports with the doctor and one of the assistant trainers—a fit guy named Josh I haven't worked with much before—and do some physical tests.

"This really necessary?" I grunt as I lift progressive weights while Josh watches and the doctor makes notes on his tablet.

"Unfortunately." He grimaces. "I get it. When I was injured at division finals for high school, it felt like all I did were tests."

"Yeah? How'd that work out?"

"You tell me." He shakes his head. "You're the one playing ball on an NBA team's payroll and I'm the one helping you rehab."

"Fair enough. But I wasn't injured," I remind him.

"Your body was. Just because you didn't tear a muscle or strain a joint doesn't mean otherwise."

His rebuke has me groaning internally.

When I'm done, I head to the weight room. We

don't officially have practice for another few days, but Rookie's there, plus Clay and Jay.

"There he is," Atlas crows.

"Never had a chance to properly congratulate you," Rookie adds.

"If you wanted to hang out at some billionaire's penthouse, there was an easier way."

We exchange fist bumps, and I take up a spot by the leg press, ready to work in when Atlas finishes.

"Are you going to tell us what happened?" Atlas asks.

"Someone hit my drink with ketamine."

Whistles and groans go up.

"That happened to a friend of mine in college," Rookie says. "It was a prank."

As a guy who pulls more than my share of those, I can see it happening. It's probably what happened to me.

"Made for a pretty good night, actually," Rookie goes on.

"I'm telling you guys. I didn't sign up for that."

That's what I didn't want—for my teammates to think I did it on purpose.

"You know me, right?" I look around the room to grudging nods.

Relieved, I shift into the rig and lower the plates.

Fuck, this is hard. *Am I weaker?*

"So, getting your drink spiked is what you blame this on?" Atlas holds up his phone with a video of me dancing in the club.

I'm sweating but find a grin as his joke slices through what's left of the tension. "Those are some serious dance moves."

"Seriously weak."

I finish the rep, plus two more.

"So is Hawkins nicer in person?" Rookie asks as I step out so Atlas can swap in.

"Nah, he's even more of a prick," I say.

"Did you see what he said on social?" Damon pulls up a clip from what looks like a podcast interview with Hawkins.

"Garrett was definitely partying hard. But cut him slack—it's his first time, and he doesn't know any better."

I'm starting to see why Jay has it in for this guy.

"We need to bury him and Boston," Jay decides.

I turn to Jay and Clay. "Brooke said you were at the hospital. Thanks for being there."

Jay nods. "Brooke was stuck to your side the entire time. I haven't seen her that stressed since school."

"I didn't mean to worry her."

His eyes cloud. "If you make my sister cry, I don't care that we need your shooting to get to the playoffs.

You're going to be *begging* to feel as bad as you did in that hospital bed."

He crosses the room to another machine, and I rub both hands over my face.

I want to tell him there's nothing I want more than keeping Brooke happy.

Speaking of which, Valentine's Day is this weekend, and I've been trying to think of what to do for her. It has to be special, but I've discarded each idea that's come up so far.

"What did you do for Nova your first Valentine's Day?" I ask Clay.

"You seriously asking me for what to get your girl."

"It's inspiration, not imitation," I promise.

Still, my teammate flushes under his tattoos. "Top secret."

Fine. Whatever.

"It's just that I've known her for years, you know? Since we started hanging out, I bought her a phone. A few, actually. Clothes. But nothing seems like enough. I want to do something special." I'm thinking of the hot air balloon ride we took on the morning of her sorority retreat.

"But there's no one who likes clothes more than Brooke," Rookie points out.

A lightbulb goes off. "You're right."

BROOKE

"Does your face hurt yet? From all the smiling?"

My mom cuts me a look. "First-time politicians think you have to get voters to fall in love with you. You don't."

"You mean you don't have to outrun a bear—you just have to be faster than the other guys?"

A gust of wind blows across the path in front of us, and she wraps her scarf more tightly around her.

Mom is the one who got me started hiking. When I was young, she had precious little free time. Now, she has less, but it still feels like being with her out here is better than being cooped up in some office. The natural environment takes the edge off.

"It's about time you came to me," she says, keeping up with me easily.

"I've been busy."

We got back to Denver yesterday, and I'm committed to making a decision about Chloe's job offer. But, all the chaos with Miles these past few days has meant I haven't had a second to think about it.

"With that Vivaro company?"

"I'm not working for them." I fill her in on their investigation.

"You did the right thing," she says, surprising me. "If only you'd put as much effort into your own business you did into the campaigns you used to help with."

"I guess I liked helping you more than myself."

I take a breath and refocus what I wanted to talk to her about.

I debated how much I should confide in her. But my mom's an expert at dealing with all sorts of crises. Despite having an entire team around her, she's a one-woman Olivia Pope and Associates.

"He had ketamine in his system."

She pulls up and turns toward me, her styled brows drawing together. "He should know better than—"

"He does," I insist.

Miles wouldn't take a party drug, not even at all-star weekend when he had a few days off to unwind.

Someone slipped it into his drink.

"You think it was an accident," she reads.

"What else?"

It could have been anyone—a fan, another club-goer? A party drug intended for someone else?

Probably. But the worst part is not knowing.

Harrison King reviewed the security footage himself and couldn't find any evidence.

It's strange and probably a fluke, but it's frustrating anyway.

She considers. "Miles Garrett might have millions of fans but his stock is about to tumble. You should distance yourself."

"It wasn't his fault," I say sharply as she starts to continue along the trail. "He's not someone you can look down on, Mom. We're dating."

She flinches. "Being caught up in a public fight is bad for business. Toppling like a giant redwood in the middle of a nightclub and getting wheeled into an ambulance is worse."

Her words are tossed over her shoulder, carried away on the wind as she starts back along the trail with a grimace.

I stomp after her. "You'd rather I was dating your favorite donor's son, wouldn't you?" My frustration escapes in cold puffs of breath. "You care more about your political wins than about my happiness."

"No, dearest. Men like Kevin can be controlled. You find out what motivates them, and you use it."

She makes it sound simple. As if every curveball life throws at her is manageable if only she's smart and careful.

Resentment builds up in my chest. "I need to tell

you something," I start. "Back in college, the drugs my sorority sister found in my room were Kevin's. They weren't mine. He wanted me to go down for it, was going to let me do it."

She pulls up ahead of me. The expression on her face is tired and a little irritated. "I know."

My mouth falls open. "You knew this the entire time? And yet you still wanted me to date him?"

She shakes her head. "His family has a deal in the works that would make them even more power-ful. With power comes responsibility."

"That's a Spider-Man quote, Mom."

Her sigh echoes off the trees. "Do you know how I met his parents?" I'm not sure how it matters, but she's already continuing. "His family's law firm has been operating for generations. His brother was a board member on a cause I supported. He was impli-cated in some abuse-of-funds charges. He used to be a partner in the firm. They cut him out and all but disowned him. Quietly, of course, privately. He died by suicide a few years later."

I feel a pang of grief. Kevin had mentioned his brother's death to me but never wanted to talk about it.

"Well, nothing happened to him after he tried to frame me in school. There were zero consequences."

"I wouldn't be quick to assume that," she says.

What consequences could there have been? I suppose we were broken up at the time, but whatever punishment Kevin suffered or didn't is none of my concern. There are bigger issues than whether he got his wrist slapped.

"In any case, the campaign has been working overtime to distance us from your 'boyfriend' and his incident," Mom says.

"I'm sorry we're costing you money."

"It's not the money. I'm concerned."

Mom never says she's worried because worrying sounds as though you're out of control.

But she's scared. She doesn't know how to manage this.

As much as I want to tell her off, I can't bring myself to do it.

I take a breath. "It was an accident. Miles wasn't doing drugs. None of our friends do. You can sleep at night."

We walk in silence for a few minutes.

"The campaign is having a dinner next week." Her words tilting up at the end. It's her good cop voice, not her bad cop one. "It would be good if you were there."

"There are people you still trust me to charm despite my problematic choices?" My voice is drier than crisp leaves clustered in snowless patches of the trail.

"You can sit with whomever you like. I'll make sure my assistant has a note of it."

I turn that over.

I do want to help her. She makes a genuine difference in the world, provides hope and opportunities for a lot of women, and works tirelessly to do it.

Plus, I can solve this Kevin problem myself.

9
____

BROOKE

When I enter the condo, two suitcases rest by the door—both mine. Already packed, my coat hanging on one of them.

When I moved in, I knew there would be an expiry date on my living here. I had put one on it myself in the form of the calendar I'd crossed days off on for an entire month.

But since we started hooking up, I'd forgotten that this wasn't really my home.

My stomach free-falls.

Waffles trots over from his bed in the corner, looking between me and the luggage as if asking the same question I am.

When Miles appears in sweatpants and no shirt, no bags in sight, it deepens my unease.

"What's all this?" I ask, trying to sound casual.

He bends to scratch Waffles's ears, looking relaxed as anything. "Valentine's Day. I wanted to go big."

"Eviction?"

He laughs as he straightens. "A date. One with a little commute."

The knot in my gut loosens, and I can breathe again. Now I'm intrigued—by the possibilities and the boyish grin on his face. "You planned a travel date?" There are two days left before the season resumes.

"I got us tickets to New York Fashion Week."

My jaw drops. "Are you joking?"

I've never been because the timing didn't work out between school and other commitments, but it's always been a dream.

"Nope." Miles crosses to me and cups my face. "I wanted to do better than the club after the all-star game. My memory of that night is spotty at best. Please tell me I wasn't a huge asshole."

I pretend to consider. "Only a moderate asshole."

"Fuck." Miles rubs a hand over his face. "I'm sorry. I bet you didn't have sitting by my bed for two days in your plans for the week. I heard you never left my side."

"All kinds of crazy things can happen to a defenseless man in Vegas."

"Well, I'm glad you happened to me first, Brooke Ellis." His crooked grin makes my heart skip.

No one has ever been this thoughtful before. Everyone asks me to do things for them—Kevin, my sorority sisters, my mom, even my brother.

"Speaking of which, I'm feeling exceptionally well rested," he goes on.

I lift my chin, brushing my fingers along the stubble of his jaw. "Then you'll be able to practice with the team as planned."

"Not thinking about the team right now."

A little shiver ripples across my skin.

Since we first got together, the longest we've gone without hooking up was a four-day road trip. I was seriously distracted and, according to Miles, he was in "actual hell."

At least we had video calls to tide us over.

Over the past week, I've been deliberately cautious around him physically because he was supposed to be recovering. He's been trying to drag me into bed with him, and I've resisted, insisting he's supposed to rest so he can get back to playing ball.

His phone rings, and he glances at it. "Agent," he says and answers it.

I play with Waffles while Miles talks.

When he hangs up, his smile is gone.

"I can't go to New York today."

"You can't come on our date?" It should be impossible for a girl who thought she was getting evicted or dumped or both two minutes ago to sound this incredulous.

"We have to meet my shoe sponsor this morning."

I turn it over. "Then we won't go. I don't want to spend it without you."

He scoops me up in his arms and kisses me. I thread my fingers into his hair.

"I have an idea. Take Ruby. I'll meet you there once I'm done."

"You got that great idea while you were kissing me?"

"I get a lot of great ideas when I'm kissing you."

"I HOPE this is up to your standards."

"I was covered in blood six hours ago. This is very civilized," Ruby says as we get up from the first fashion show, collecting the gift bags we got when we entered. She turns over a makeup compact in her hand. "Givenchy? Nice."

We head for a cute lounge that's already packed

thanks to the week's activities. Ruby shifts onto a seat at a high-top table. Her black pantsuit is perfectly chic. No matter what she says about living in scrubs, she cleans up impeccably.

"Did you decide about the new job?" I arrange myself on a stool across from my friend and we order drinks. It's fun to get dressed up and rub shoulders with a fashionable set.

"I'm going to take it."

"That's amazing!"

"I'm finishing out the month here, then I'll start in March with the new role. I'm still afraid it will eat into my already-limited free time."

Around us, tables of patrons buzz. I catch snippets of conversation—behind us, magazine editors are discussing a new shoot.

"If you were a guy, you wouldn't even think about it."

"I know, but I'm not. I want to spend time with my kids."

"Tim's going to have to man up and do more."

"That's what I'm hoping. How about you? Are you working on any new brand partnerships?"

I sip my drink. "With Vivaro still investigating internally, whatever that means, it's harder to land deals. I don't have regular money coming in."

As generous as Miles has been, insisting he can

cover both our living expenses, I want to pay my own way.

"I'm still thinking about this job Chloe offered me with the Kodiaks," I say.

"I bet a lot of people would love to work with the world champions. Does working for the team excite you?"

We're surrounded by people collaborating, friends and colleagues from all over the world, all at the top of their game and thrilled to be here and doing what they're passionate about. They're carving out new directions, breaking new ground.

"Yes and no," I say. "It's a good opportunity. It's not as if I have dozens of job offers."

Ruby frowns. "The most enthusiastic I've seen you was working on campaigns for the Kappas, or hearing you talk about Nova's art career. One of the reasons I knew we'd be friends was because you cared about contributing to a cause that was bigger than yourself."

"I thought it was because there were hardly any Black girls and we had the same taste in shoes."

She laughs. "It does help, having that conviction you're making a difference. When the days are rough, I remind myself of a patient I helped who would have been worse off otherwise."

"The exhaustion melts away?" I ask wryly,

though my heart warms at the thought of how my friend helps people.

"No. But it feels good enough that when the alarm goes off the next morning, I get up." My friend winks. "When is Miles getting in?"

"Landing at five. He's meeting me for dinner. I haven't heard how his sponsor call went."

"How are things going? You're living together and dating in the open. That's a big deal."

I bite my lip. "It was easier back when we were sneaking around—before he got his shoe deal and named to the all-star game, and before I took up this cause as the defender of online creators or whatever."

"You've got big-girl problems now, like what happened after the all-star game." She cocks her head. "I was worried about you guys."

I tell her about the ketamine they found in Miles's system.

"You think someone drugged him?" Ruby's gaze sharpens. "I see it all the time. People come into the ER. It's too easy."

"It could have been an accident. Right?"

"Sure." Ruby's mouth parts. "What does Miles think happened?"

"He brushes it off. I think he wants so badly to get back to normal. We haven't really talked about it."

My big sis folds her arms. "Maybe it's time you do."

"Holy hell."

Miles's reaction is worth every second I spent getting my hair and makeup done before our date. My hair is half pinned up, the rest falling in waves down my back. My dress ends high on my thighs, and my four-inch heels mean I barely have to tilt up my chin to meet his gaze as I lean back against the side of the limo.

"You clean up good, Princess."

I take him in as he crosses the distance between us. His cocky smile is sexy as sin.

He looks delicious himself, his lean legs clad in dark jeans. A zip-up knit sweater a few shades darker than his eyes clings to strong shoulders, the hard planes of his chest and abs. His jaw is sharp, his hair waving across his forehead.

A few passengers outside the airport recognize him, pointing as they pass. A couple snap discreet pics.

"Miles Garrett!" one calls.

He offers a quick wave and a genuine smile.

My heart kicks. I love that he makes time for his fans, that none of it's fake.

"We could go directly to the hotel. Forget the event," Miles murmurs against my neck as he turns back to me.

I pretend to debate. "But I'm hungry."

"Me too." His eyes glint wickedly.

"What does Miles think happened?" Ruby's words play in my head.

Now that Miles is here, I realize how much stress we've both been under.

Miles's grin settles on me. For the first time in days, he looks genuinely happy.

I won't let Ruby's question into our date, our night.

"You're having a good season. Don't lose focus!" a fan calls from behind him.

His smile doesn't falter, but I know he clocks it as he takes my hand and tugs me into the back of the limo.

Every day, hour, second, we've been apart this week feels as if it piles on me at once. It's more than the distance—it's the added worry I've been feeling about him, wanting to fix it but not being able to.

He pulls me into his lap and kisses me, hard and deep. His palm slides up my thigh.

"We should really go back to the hotel." His words are a throaty promise.

Maybe we should, judging from the way his fingers on the back of my neck make heat pool in my stomach.

"This party has some up-and-coming designers." I moan against his mouth as my hands tangle in his hair. "Plus, I already gave the driver the address."

"Well, fuck. What're we going to do?" he groans.

My body is already humming with him, vibrating with need.

His touch is filled with urgency. The laid-back Miles Garrett from a moment ago, smiling at fans, is gone. This version is even sexier, because he's completely strung out over me.

"Can we..." I trail off as his hand slips between my thighs and brushes where I'm throbbing.

Miles buzzes down the partition and tears his mouth from mine. I think he's about to argue when he says, "Take the long way."

"It's Manhattan, sir. Every way is the long way."

Miles chuckles as he buzzes the divider back up.

"Now we have a minute to catch up." His hands grip my hips as he shifts me to straddle him. The dress tugs against my thighs, riding up around my ass. "How was your day?"

"That's what you wanted to do when you got me alone." My hand fists in his sweater as I take him in.

"Mhmm. I want to know everything." Miles's fingers shift up my thighs, tugging my legs farther apart. Pleasure spikes through me as I rest on him, feeling him already hard through his jeans and the thin fabric of my panties.

"My boyfriend got me and my friend tickets to Fashion Week and flew here in time to meet me for dinner. Yours?"

"Got through a dry as hell meeting about logistics and projections and bonuses."

I love that Miles thinks talking about money is boring.

"Been thinking about you for hours," he groans.

Satisfaction blooms deep within me, twining with nowhere-near-satiated need.

"Only hours?" I work the button open and the fly down on his jeans.

His breathing gets shallow. "Days. Months. Fucking years I've been thinking of you, Princess."

Emotion and need war in my chest.

His fingers slide beneath my thong. Pleasure collides with feelings that are stronger, more powerful, than any I've felt.

"Hate to mess you up," he groans as he tugs it and

my bra down, his thumbs grazing my nipples. "You look like you belong here."

My heart kicks. "I've had people my entire life tell me I don't look like I belong. I know deep down that I do, but I get tired of reminding myself."

His lips brush mine. "You're a fucking queen, Brooke Ellis." When they come back again, they cling, and I lose myself in the taste of him.

"I was worried about you this week," I admit when we part an inch.

He groans. "I'm sorry. I think being there got inside my head a little. I can't take it back, but I can show you I'm here now, that we're okay. Sound good?"

I nod slowly.

"I like you dressed up, but..." He reaches for the pins in my hair. "I like you even better dressed down."

Miles waits for permission. He knows how important it is to me to look put together—that I'm not sure who I am when I can't control the narrative.

"Do it."

Without asking twice, he yanks fistfuls of pins out of my hair, drags my lips against his, and devours me with hunger.

Yes. This is what I want. The need, the storm.

But more than that, it's knowing that he sees me, that he believes in me and has my back.

It's *everything*.

His fingers slid between us, inside me.

Every thought flies out of my head. Pleasure spirals through me, starting at my core and spinning out into a need that's all-consuming. How is it possible to be so satisfied and so needy at once? I never knew it was possible before this man. This moment.

I need more of him. All of him.

He groans against my mouth. His other hand grips my ass, grinding me down on him.

He's already so deep, and it's only his fingers. It's true what they say about big hands, but he also knows how to use them. It's as if someone gave him a playbook of exactly how to make me writhe.

"Come on me," he groans. "Come on me and I'll fuck you properly."

Miles pulls back long enough to add a third finger. I arch against him, inhaling sharply at the feel of him. The scent of him, of us, fills the car. He rubs his thumb across my clit, and I'm so close.

I explode, crying out as my arms tighten around his neck.

"That's it, Princess. So beautiful."

He waits for me to come back to Earth, my damp

forehead pressed against his neck. But I'm aware of his cock between us, twitching. I'm satisfied, but it's not enough.

My hips arch, sliding lazily over him.

Miles's laugh is tortured. "How long do you think you can do that for?"

"Long as I want," I say tartly.

His tip slips inside, making me gasp. He grabs my arms and shifts me back. "Wait. Condom."

The reaction is automatic. But as I watch him search his pockets, looking rumpled and determined and increasingly desperate, a better idea forms.

"Or... we could not."

He stills, all that attention going straight back onto me. "You sure?"

There's not enough air in the limo. A second ago we were fine, but there's a weight on my chest, my lungs.

I don't leave myself exposed with anyone. But with Miles, I'm not trying to scratch an itch.

I don't only want him. I want us.

"So sure," I whisper.

We've talked before about having been tested since either of us was with anyone else.

The way his face transforms...

He positions me over him, the head of his cock

teasing me as I rock back and forth. Then he tugs me down.

Oh, damn.

Anyone who says size is all that matters is full of shit, but the feeling of him filling me, stretching me, coupled with the tug in my chest when he looks in my eyes, is beyond anything I've ever experienced.

"Fuck, you take me so good." He groans, kneading my ass. "So tight and wet with nothing between us."

"I dreamed about this one night," I confess.

"I dream about this every night."

At first, I'm riding him, but soon he's lifting and lowering me.

In this car, there are no cameras. There's no Kevin or my mom. Nothing and no one can get inside.

My nails rake under his sweater and T-shirt, making his skin shiver as his abs flex. I squeeze him, hard. He hisses out a breath and shoots me a look like he knows exactly what I'm doing.

"Oh, that's how we're going to do this? You want me to come first?"

"Only fair," I murmur.

Then he hooks a hand under my knee, lifting it so my shin presses his chest. "Agree to disagree, Princess."

He pulls out and strokes back in. I gasp. The new angle makes the fit even tighter. He just upped the ante.

"Don't stop now," he challenges, a tight grin on his face.

I grind against him, taking him as deep as I can. I want to make him come, but it's dangerous work. Everything I do to torment him only brings me closer to the edge.

The feel of him is exquisite. Combined with our damp skin, the scent of his aftershave, his low rasping breath, and him stroking my clit, I'm nearly lost to pleasure.

Then the next stroke, he trembles a little. I sense my advantage and tug his lip between my teeth, feeling him twitch inside me.

"You know you want to," I murmur against his lips.

"Almost as much as you do." His thumb presses where I'm sensitive.

It's a war, one I'd die to fight.

"Together?" he offers.

I try to hold out an extra second but fail. When his muscles clench and I feel him spurt inside me, I gasp into his neck as my own climax overtakes me.

"What did you in?" I ask as my heart rate comes back down a little.

"The realization that you're going to feel me inside you all night." His wicked grin makes my breath catch. He hesitates. "Brooke, for real, that was incredible."

"Yeah, it was." I'm still breathless, but it's from being near him as much as from what we just did. "You're going to need a change of clothes."

"Brought one in my bag in case." Miles eyes the space around us doubtfully.

"You'd get changed in the back of a limo for me?" I tease.

His lips twitch as his gaze flicks back to mine. "I'd do anything for you."

"Look who it is." Elise cuts through the crowd, eyes wide with sincere surprise.

The party is being hosted at a SoHo loft by a big magazine editor. I didn't expect to run into Elise here.

"You look wonderful."

"You too." I'm flushed, my hair cascading around my face, but my lipstick is on point.

"You're going to feel me inside you all night."

He wasn't wrong. As I shift on my feet, I feel the first ache from what we did.

I don't look at Miles, but I sense him at my side.

"I'll give you ladies a second," he says, brushing his lips over my cheek. "Let me know if you need backup."

"Thanks." I shoot him a look of sincere gratitude.

Miles heads to the bar, where he's instantly accosted. He gamely agrees to snap a couple of selfies.

"Your new line is stunning. How are things going with your new brand rep?" I ask.

Her smile fades a little. "I suppose it's somewhat ironic that you two are still together while Caroline's relationship was called off."

I don't even try to look surprised, as though I didn't hear about Caroline and Kevin. "If you're rethinking what you decided about us collaborating..."

She laughs. "That's jumping from one problem to another. With partnerships, you're tying yourself to another person and their opinions and everyone else around them. I understand you boyfriend is still a contentious figure."

"Why?" I'm startled that she still sees Miles that way.

Elise makes a noncommittal shrug. "My husband said he made headlines for partying."

I start to argue, but stop myself. There's no point. The media will make of it what they want.

"So what, I should convince you Caroline is worse?" I ask lightly.

"Do you want to?"

There are a dozen things I could point out from the way Caroline's treated me in the past, but I still feel for her getting dumped and I'm tired of feeding into some narrative, real or fake.

"No. I think she cares about your brand, and when she cares, she's very motivated," I say.

"That's decent of you," Elise says after a moment. "If there's anything I can do to help you, let me know."

I think fast since I'm not sure when I'll see my former sorority sister next and land on Nova's new work. "I'm helping a friend structure new partnership agreements, and I wonder if you'd be willing to share some examples from your business. From one Kappa to another."

This time, there's no hesitation. "Follow up with Sarah on my team. I'll send you her number."

I swap cheek kisses with Elise and watch her disappear into the crowd.

I go in search of my boyfriend. I find him inspecting a silver gown on a mannequin. "Bridal collection," I offer.

"It's moody."

"It's a risk," I agree. "Let me guess—you hate it."

"It's the only wedding dress I've ever looked twice at, so apparently not."

I try to push the conversation with Elise from my mind. "You want to get married someday, Garrett?"

He's quiet. "If you'd asked me a year ago, I would've said no."

I think back to what he told me about his parents and their divorce—how he ended up the ammunition in their hostile war.

"And now?"

The question shouldn't feel loaded, but it does. Suddenly, I'm picturing me walking down the aisle, and I was never the little girl who imagined those things.

I'm exposed again, more so than being naked in the limo.

Because I'm afraid he'll think that's what I want.

I'm afraid I'll realize it's what I do want.

"Maybe."

My heart skips.

"I thought marriage made people worse versions of themselves," he says. "I couldn't see a relationship making people better."

I take a few steps around the gown, taking in the beautiful details. It's unique and striking.

"What if relationships don't make people better or worse, they only expose more of who you truly are?"

He frowns, oddly serious for once. "Then I'd choose to be with someone who sees as much of me as possible and likes me anyway. And I'd want to see every part of them."

Standing on a pedestal next to the gown is a bouquet full of anemones, their white petals soft around a deep blue center.

"Including their cracks?"

"Yeah. I mean, the cracks are where the flowers grow." Miles reaches behind me to lift a flower from the vase and hold it out.

"Pretty sure that's not allowed."

A half smile plays on his lips. "I won't tell if you don't."

My breath catches as I take it from him.

"Every girl and half the guys in here would be happy to be with you. Even before you started talking like that."

Miles is handsome and fun but what no one sees is how startlingly sweet he is. How thoughtful and caring.

He wraps an arm around me and holds up his phone, snapping a photo.

"What was that for?"

"Show 'em I'm with you." He posts it to social and tags me with a flower and a blue heart emoji. "Best place I've ever been, by the way," he adds.

"You've played in an all-star game."

"Said what I said."

My heart does a little flip.

If there's a casual response to that, I don't know what it is.

He's taken me prisoner with a grin and a flower, with his admissions that he's always cared when other people treated me as disposable after getting what they wanted.

Going to the all-star game in his jersey and being seen at the club with him weren't exactly being inconspicuous, but we've yet to fan the flames of speculation. This photo and caption are definitely going to do it.

"You ever want to reinvent yourself?" The words slip out before I can question them.

"All the time." His earnest answer has me cutting a surprised look his way. "I love basketball, but don't get me wrong, I dream about what else I want to do. When I was a kid, I wanted to be a zoologist. I think my chances are gone, but I hear you can still swim with the dolphins. What about you?"

"I wanted to be a surfer."

He laughs, his bright eyes dancing.

I would feel embarrassed saying that to anyone else, but with him, I'm willing to take the heat. "I watched this competition once as a kid, and it looked so badass. Being one with nature, having it kick your ass until you learn to ride it... But I never spent enough time by the ocean, and it definitely wasn't on the list of acceptable careers. There was no way to major in surfing in college. Now that I'm a grown-ass adult..."

I should be over it.

"You can do whatever the fuck you want," he finishes.

Miles takes the flower back from me and tucks it gently behind my ear, sliding the stem into my hair before lowering his hands.

"We could do it, you know. The surfing. The swimming with the dolphins. We could do it together."

His gaze searches mine.

I'm thinking about all-star weekend, recovering in the hotel room.

I'm thinking about someone doing that to him, possibly on purpose.

I'm thinking about how I can't help being the person who thinks about those things.

"Yeah, we could," I say.

10

MILES

"They give you a lifetime supply?" Rookie marvels as I pull up to my locker at the arena and drop the three shoe boxes in front of it.

Each pair is a different color, each with my name stitched across the heel. They're all for me to use in tonight's game.

The past few days, I've been trying to get back into a rhythm. A payment arrived at my bank from my sponsor, and the bulk of it went directly into an account for Grams.

But since Vegas, James made it clear I'm on a tight leash.

"You're popular with the fan base and you're having a great season, both of which Chloe keeps reminding me.

But try anything else cute and you'll be facing more than an apology."

I hand Rookie a pair of the shoes, then stash my phone and keys on the top shelf of my locker. Besides my uniform and some gym gear, I don't keep a lot of stuff in here.

Today, I stick a picture of Brooke inside.

It's one I took of her on a sleepy weekend morning. She's smiling, her arms around Waffles as he licks her face.

At this stage in the season, chemistry within the team is more important than ever, but I'm not going to dance around the fact that we're together.

Rookie glances in my locker, his gaze lingering on the photo before he slips on the shoes. "Looks like I've got bigger feet than you." He grins. "Tell your girl."

I laugh. "She's not interested."

"In all this?" He gestures to his body. "Find that hard to believe."

A towel lands on his head. "Hey. That's my sister you're talking about," Jay says.

"I'm not the one who's—"

I grab Rookie's shoulder, and he looks at me, caught out.

"The one sleeping—"

Jay snarls. My head tilts as I press my thumb under Rookie's shoulder blade.

"Respectfully! Sleeping respectfully."

I step back, and so does Jay.

He notices the photo and freezes.

So much for chemistry.

Stillness descends over the entire locker room until it feels as if everyone's afraid to breathe.

"Heard you went to New York," Jay says finally. "She's always wanted to go to Fashion Week."

A breath whooshes out of me, and the rest of the guys go back to their tasks.

The way my friend and captain's acting, he might be slowly coming around to the idea that we're together.

Aside from Clay, most of my teammates don't have serious relationships, but I want Brooke in my life. The way she's had my back this past week was one more reminder of why.

Rookie cuts a look at the clock. "How many trade deadlines pass without any changes?"

That's the real reason the team is walking on eggshells. The entire day, we've been on edge. Even if management says you're safe, it's never a done deal until the time elapses.

"Not many," Clay says evenly.

"It's part of the game," Damon agrees.

Each team in the league is trying to make itself as strong as possible with just over a month until the postseason, and we're still a spot out of where we need to be.

From the early problems of the season with Atlas out to me "overperforming"—the stats guys' words, not mine—it's been a battle back and forth for us to grab the playoff spot we deserve. The one that we frankly expected to, even if half the world thinks we were lucky last year.

Every guy in here has an alert on his phone for any moves. If it sounds brutal that you'd find out you're traded from a notification on a major news outlet, you're not wrong. We commit all of ourselves to fitting into a team, making the biggest difference we can as though it's our home forever.

And it is—right up until some suit decides you're a chess piece worth swapping on a wild hunch.

"You ever get traded at deadline?" Rookie asks me.

I shake my head. It never bothered me before, so I never thought about it much.

Except that if it happened today, I have no idea what I'd do.

I mean, I'd pack a bag and get on a plane because that's what you have to do.

But what about Brooke? Would she go with me? Could I even ask her?

It feels like our weekend in New York brought us closer together, but I don't think we're at "please move across the country with me" status yet.

There've been a couple of big moves across the league so far but nothing involving the Kodiaks.

Could be indicative of the final shakedown, or it could be the calm before the storm.

James warning echoes in my head.

Half an hour.

The minutes slip away as we get ready for shootaround.

Out on the court, fans trickle in as Dallas warms up at the other end.

Assistant trainers feed us balls, and we take turns shooting layups and threes. Each time one swishes through the hoop, it eases the tension in my gut a little, but when I glance up toward the spot where Harlan and James sit, neither is there. Probably in their offices on the phone, deciding all our fates.

There's no time to dwell on it. Not when we have a game to focus on that's going to shape what kind of team anyone who's staying will come home to.

"All-star break is over," Coach says when we're all back in the locker room doing final prep. "Back to work, only double the intensity. This is what you train your entire lives for. Make it happen."

Dallas is above us in the standings, and we're on the hunt for a playoff spot. We need to claw our way back into a strong position.

The top six teams are guaranteed a spot in playoffs. Seven and eight have to play their way in against stronger opponents. While on paper we'd have a shot at seven or eight, we need to be six or better.

"We've got this," Jay says, leveling his gaze at me. "Kodiaks on three."

The team puts in their hands. After our cheer, we file out of the locker room.

I call for Jay on the way out to the court, and he hangs back.

"How're you feeling?"

"Good. Normal," I say and almost mean it.

"I'd understand if you weren't. Ketamine can fuck you up."

I nod. "I don't want to go there again."

He eyes me a long time before clapping a hand on my shoulder. "No shit."

Maybe Clay has it right avoiding alcohol during the season. From here on out, things are going to be better. I'll be a model athlete.

We head out side by side for the player announcements.

When the crowd goes crazy for us, adrenaline surges through me and blanks out everything else. I look up to the box to see Brooke and Nova, plus Sierra. Chloe's absent—probably with Harlan and James.

Brooke's laughing with her friends, and when her gaze finds mine, she tilts her chin at me.

My heart pounds harder.

She's here for me.

I've had women come mainly to watch me play. Hell, judging from the fans wearing my jerseys, it's a regular occurrence.

But I'd trade a thousand fans for one.

For her.

We're playing an afternoon game, and Brooke said she has to drop in on a dinner her mom's having, so I won't catch her until later.

But looking at my girl fuels me.

The rush of feelings from New York come back.

I meant it when I said I'd do anything for her. When we talked about our dreams, I could picture her there with me. I've never wanted anything so badly.

I love her, and I'm going to tell her.

Tonight.

WHETHER IT'S her presence or being back on home court, the first quarter is the best I've felt in weeks. With Atlas back, I can combine my new game with my old one—showing up around the perimeter for a three, cutting into the paint when the opportunity presents itself.

Second quarter is tough, but we sneak into half-time still in the lead.

The clock expires on the trade deadline, and the guys high-five and fist-bump down the bench.

"Still here," Jay calls.

The starters all look at one another. "Still here."

Clay straightens, unzipping his warmup jacket. "Let's send Dallas back home with claw marks."

Cheers go up.

No one can stop this team. We're a family. A unit.

Third and fourth quarters are gritty, but Jay's moving the ball with extra pop. I'm back to pre-all-star form. Clay fills in gaps in his MVP form. Atlas is big at the net, and even Rookie finds spots to shine.

We get the win, and we're pumped.

"Fuck yeah. Playoffs, here we come!" Jay hollers, wrapping an arm around my neck.

After, when I get back to the locker room, Chloe's by the door.

"We got the win, Chlo. Look happier," Jay says as he breezes toward her.

She turns her attention to me but grips her iPad tighter. "Miles. We need a word." Jay starts to head into the locker room, but Chloe holds up a slim arm to bar his entrance. "Only Garrett."

"The fuck is going on?" Jay looks between us.

She nods toward the locker room.

When I get into the room, I pull up. Harlan and James are standing by my locker. Security is with them.

"There something you want to tell us?" Harlan asks.

I look between them. "What?" The adrenaline from the game is still pounding in my veins.

"We found drugs in your locker."

11

———

BROOKE

The Kodiaks's win was electric. They needed it, and the entire town is buzzing.

By the time it's over, the last thing I want to do is stop by a public event for my mom, but it's too late to back out.

Plus, I have work to do.

I took an Uber across town, pausing when I got out at the bus stop featuring a full-height poster of the team. Miles is right next to Clay wearing a shit-eating grin.

I blow poster Miles a kiss.

The dinner is at a restaurant, held in a private room. A couple dozen supporters are here to network and cut checks. At this point in the campaign, my mom's track record is important, but exposure matters more, and donations help get her name out.

"Brooke, how lovely to see you." One of mom's donors smiles from next to bar, a glass of champagne in her hand. "How have you been?"

I get a glass of wine and we catch up for a few minutes. She tells me about her daughters, both in school and trying to decide what they want to be. She's starting a program to grow scholarships for women in business.

"Kevin," she says after, her gaze flicking past me.

I try not to inhale is cologne as I turn to find him next to me.

"Ladies." His suit is perfectly pressed, his teeth flashing white. It's like someone popped him brand new out of a protective box outside the restaurant and sent him inside.

"I hear congratulations are in order," the woman continues.

"Thank you. The merger isn't a done deal, but my father's been working on it for years."

"I meant your engagement. How is Caroline?" the other donor asks.

Kevin smiles. "Busy."

The answer takes me by surprise. Not "we broke up," no "unfortunately the engagement is off."

I cock my head. "Busy? Doing what?"

He doesn't miss a beat. "Philanthropy mostly. She's very involved."

The woman gets pulled away and I lower my voice. "So, you're split, but you haven't told anyone?"

Kevin frowns. "We're not advertising it."

I'm used to everyone hiding things, but this is next level. "You could have just stayed engaged."

"Hardly." He sighs. "You have any idea how dull it is to be around someone who wants to give you exactly what you want?"

He's unbelievable. "Do your parents not keep you busy enough at the firm that you have to keep tabs on my boyfriend and me?"

He leans a shoulder against the wall, looking past me. "I'm sure I don't know what you're talking about."

"You came at Miles at the Kodiaks' arena. He doesn't owe you anything. You both acted like assholes in college as far as I'm concerned."

"But he's the idiot you want to be with?" He grins, the smile I used to find charming.

"It sounds like you have a family merger you should be focused on." I lift my glass to my lips and take a long sip. Then two more.

"You're right," he says after a moment. "I shouldn't have confronted Garrett. I was bitter and I wanted to prove something to myself. After what happened in college, it took a long time to earn my family's trust back. We handled it internally, but I promise that I've spent a lot of time thinking about it. And I'm sorry for the pain I've caused you."

I nearly choke on the wine. "You're sorry," I echo.

"Yes. But Brooke, let me tell you something." He leans in, urgency written across his smooth features. "If you're smart—and I know you are—you won't cast your lot in with him. He might act like he cares, but you'll be the one left picking up the pieces."

There's soft music streaming from a speaker in the corner of the room. I let a few bars of it wash over me before I respond.

"Your problem, Kevin, is that you don't know how to lose. You take it out on everyone else. Me, when I outed you for your lies. Miles, who tried to hold you accountable. Caroline, who only ever had your back. I honestly hope there's a point at which you'll feel better."

Showing desperation is always a bad idea, but it slips out before I can stop it.

Kevin cocks his head, a shadow flickering across his eyes. It's a response to my vulnerability, or maybe a trick of the light. "Me too."

He brushes his cold lips over my cheek before I can jerk away, then moves past me toward the dinner.

By the time I catch a ride from the dinner, I want to take a scalding hot bath and curl up with Miles on the couch with a TV show and popcorn. We've started watching K-dramas. I love the twisty plots and Miles is fascinated by the families and unlikely friend groups.

I've texted Miles more than once, but there's been no answer.

Weird. It's after ten, and media for the afternoon game should've wrapped hours ago.

I head up to the condo and grab Waffles, who's impatiently whining to go out for a walk.

I call my brother from the sidewalk, the Frenchie sniffing desperately around a fire hydrant.

"Jay," I say when he answers on the fourth ring. "I can't get hold of Miles. Have you seen him?"

"He's with management." His voice sounds wrong.

"Are they still upset about his apology? I told him that wouldn't work—"

"They found cocaine in his locker."

My heart plummets. "What?"

He repeats his statement.

A gust of cold wind blows through my coat, but I barely feel it.

"How could this happen?"

"I don't know, Brooke."

Waffles tugs me half a block, happily oblivious. I stumble along the sidewalk after him.

"He's a professional athlete. He's serious about his career, he wouldn't do that," I say.

There's a pause long enough I glance at my phone to see that the call is still connected.

"He is serious, but he can't say he's *never* done it."

The words land deep in my ribs, scratching like a thorn.

"What? When?"

Jay sighs. "A long time ago. Before he got drafted."

I process that. It's not wild that a kid would experiment a little, but it bothers me that he never mentioned it, especially given the issues I had with Kevin back in college, the role that drugs played.

"If Miles was taking anything now, I would know," I insist.

Wouldn't I?

There's a flicker of doubt, a question mark that makes me hate myself before I brush it aside.

Yes. Absolutely.

Waffles does his business, and I switch into cleanup mode.

"This will blow over," I say as I finish, tossing the bag in a nearby trashcan and heading back toward the condo building. "They'll drug test him. He'll be clean. It will be obvious it wasn't his."

"And someone put drugs in his locker by mistake?"

The possibility sounds ridiculous, but there aren't a lot of options.

"Or it was planted."

"Who would do that?"

"A second-string player envious of the amount of time and attention he's suddenly getting? Someone who has it in for the Kodiaks?" I counter.

The concierge holds the doors as I step inside.

"Easy, tiger. You're starting to sound like mom."

I bristle. "What are you saying?"

"Just that once is a coincidence but twice is harder to believe." He pauses. "Miles is my friend and I don't like talking behind his back. But, he has been having a career defining year. Maybe the pressure is getting to him."

Incredulity rises like steam in my throat. My heels and Waffles's nails click on the marble floors as we head for the elevator.

"I think you're still not happy about the two of us together and you're looking for problems where there aren't any." I step inside and stab a button.

He curses. "That's not it, Brooke. You know how I

know? Because I should be worried for him and the team, and I am, but I'm more worried for you."

The words set me back. "Me? Why?"

"Because I don't want you dragged down by this. Because you've been dragged down by assholes before. Because..." He swallows. "Faceless people say shit about you that's wrong and cruel and unfair, and I see how much it hurts you."

My breathing slows as I fixate on the person in the mirror.

I appreciate that he noticed. It's bittersweet, because I wish he'd said something to me years ago to let on that he saw.

"Miles isn't an asshole," I say finally. Waffles snorts in agreement.

"I know, but you being together is making your life harder, and you deserve better."

The elevator dings, announcing our floor.

I say a tense goodbye to my brother and start down the hall.

I open the condo door, not fully aware of my own reaction until I see Waffles is blurred and fuzzy through my tears.

That's when a notification pings on my phone.

The news got leaked to the press.

People are commenting on the post of the two of

us, speculating that dating me had something to do with Miles's recent troubles.

What if I have?

My ribs hurt with the dull ache of betrayal and loneliness that's as familiar as it is painful.

Waffles snuffs at my ankles, and I lift him into my arms as I kick off my shoes and head for the couch.

MILES

"Princess?" I drop my gear beside the front door and look around the condo.

It's late, or early depending on how you think about it.

The game feels like a thousand years ago. Since then, I've been dragged over the coals by management, interrogated by lawyers, and I've seen way too much of my agent's bleary face after he got dragged out of bed to come down to the stadium.

"What do you mean you found drugs in my locker?"

We're back in the conference room. This time, there are lawyers.

Harlan and James are on the same side of the table.

There's no Jay.

"A team member was putting gear in everyone's lockers and saw a suspicious substance."

"There was nothing in my locker. My keys. My phone."

James doesn't look persuaded. "When you got into a fistfight, we backed you. Then there was the incident after the all-star game—"

"Nothing happened." I say it for the millionth time.

"This is a new level of problem." Harlan's the reasonable one of the two of them, and the fact that he's not on my side anymore is sobering. "I understand that you've flown high this year, and that kind of change has a tendency to impact a person. Aside from the fact that you're violating multiple team rules, the police could charge you with possession. That would drag us into the media, which is bad for everyone."

"Surely we can deal with it internally." This is from James.

"There's nothing to deal with. Whatever you found, it's not mine," I insist.

"So, what did happen?" Harlan asks.

They stare me down, the Kodiaks' attorneys silently flanking them.

As far as the team goes, I haven't had a second to talk to any of them, but I hope to hell they have my back in this. I hate wondering what they might be thinking.

I didn't get to see the texts from my girl until way too late. At that point, I wanted to see her more than I wanted to correspond through impersonal texts.

Now, I call her name again into the empty condo.

Brooke emerges from the direction of the bedrooms.

Seeing her is a relief, soothing my stress.

"Jay told me." Her hands find my arms. Her bright-pink nails should be cheerful, but they can't erase the pit in my stomach. "I'm sorry."

Everything crashes into me at once. "It wasn't mine. Someone put it there."

"I believe you." Her dark eyes are intent on mine. "But you have used. In the past."

My chest tightens. This isn't how I wanted to tell her. This isn't how I wanted any of this to be.

"It was a long time ago," I say. "My Grams was having a hard time, my parents had split. It was a mistake and I didn't know better. I do now."

Brooke releases me and steps back.

I don't want her to look at me like that, but my mind has been spinning since management turned up coke in my locker.

"If it wasn't you, then there's a way to frame this until they get to the truth," she says. "The pressure of being the number-one option on a team can get to a person."

I pause to look at her. "That's not what's happening."

"I know, but you need a story to buy you time."

"There's not always a story, Brooke. This is my life."

Frustration rises up, all the emotions of this day concentrating as my gaze lands on the team photo I have mounted inside the door, one that Brooke had made for me.

My fist tightens and I bang it into the wall.

The frame jumps and drops to the floor, the glass shattering on the hardwood. Waffles whimpers.

Brooke pulls Waffles away from the door.

Fuck.

"I'm sorry, Princess. It's been a hell of a day."

I have to clean this up. There's a broom somewhere, but when I check the front hall closet, I don't see anything.

I stalk through my condo to check every closet. *Where is a fucking broom when you need one?*

I finally track down the broom and take it to the front hall. I sweep up the pieces of glass.

"Maybe you need some time to yourself. To process everything," she says.

"I don't need to process anything," I say, straightening with the dustpan.

One extra piece of glass glints in the light on the

floor, and I bend to retrieve it, then curse as it slices into my finger. It's barely a paper cut, but it stings, bright red blossoming on my finger.

"I care about you, and I'm telling you that you haven't been the subject of this much attention before," she tries.

Brooke reaches for my hand, but I shrug her off and head for the kitchen. I dump the glass into a trash bag and wrap it inside another.

"I've lived under the same roof with my brother," she presses. "I know how intense things get."

"It won't get intense," I say.

She reaches for my finger. I pull away, and she looks at me with surprise and regret, like the guys in the hallway when management dragged me off earlier.

"You want smooth sailing. It won't be for a while. Everyone is going to be scrutinizing you—who you spend time with, your priorities."

She's not wrong, which is why I'm silent as she continues.

"Maybe we should take a little space."

Those words snap me back. I'm not quiet now.

"Nothing's wrong with how I spend my time or who with," I say firmly.

"It's an important time for your season. You need to focus on basketball." Brooke tilts her face. "You don't have the luxury of time with the playoffs a month away."

I'm still hearing "space."

That's the opposite of what I want with her. After watching her from a distance for so long, surviving on the moments of laughing with her, touching her, wanting her in secret.

"No. Things have been fine since you moved in. My life's better with you in it."

But hers isn't. I see it on her face.

I pull up social media and scroll through. They're saying shit about me but even worse about her. They're implying I've gotten distracted since I started dating her, that she's a bad influence.

I'm the one caught out but her reputation is suffering.

It never occurred to me, but it does now.

The truth is a stabbing pain in me, worse than what I felt in that room with Harlan and James.

I take her by the shoulders, pull her toward me. On some level, I know I'm being selfish, but I want her to say that we'll figure this out. Together.

If she leaves...

There's no guarantee she'll come back.

"Miles..." Her lips lift, but there's sadness on her face. Her eyes shine with regret.

A knock on the door jars me out of my thoughts.

Brooke turns and opens it.

Jay's waiting outside. "Everything okay?" He looks between us.

"Don't go." Desperation edges in, and I reach for her hand, smearing blood on her skin.

I wouldn't be in this position if it wasn't for her. I wouldn't have had the season I've had. I wouldn't have felt as high as I've felt without this woman in my life in a way I stopped letting myself believe I could have her.

"It's not forever. Just until life settles down. I'm afraid that if I don't, you could lose everything you've worked for." Brooke's voice wavers at the edge, and it's that waver that makes me release her.

As I watch her go, with the same bags I packed for our romantic trip a week ago, I can't help thinking...

If you leave, I've already lost.

HOOPSNEWS UPDATE: KODIAKS GUARD GARRETT SUSPENDED FIVE GAMES FOLLOWING DRUG INCIDENT

12

BROOKE

"That's bullshit," Ruby declares as we walk along Huntington Pier.

"It's true. Vitamin D fixes everything." Nova takes a sip from her water bottle. "Not that kind of vitamin D," she adds at my arched brow.

The LA sunshine beats down on us, and I pull my sunglasses off my head and slide them up my nose.

Since I walked out of Miles's place, it's been a rough few days.

I moved back in with my parents. To their credit, they didn't ask what happened with Miles, and I didn't volunteer it.

I didn't take all my things because that would hurt more, would make this feel more permanent.

Instead, I brought a few bags of clothes and necessities. I can go back for the rest when I have to.

If I have to.

I didn't realize how hard it would be waking up without him. Making my own coffee sucks, and it's not only that it tastes different.

This weekend away was scheduled for a chance to visit Coastal Gallery, but I'm hoping it's also going to take the edge off.

It has to.

"We still have a couple of hours before the meeting. We could go shopping?" Nova suggests.

Two sets of eyes land on me.

"Brooke, you wake up wanting to shop," Ruby reminds me. "Even when every Kappa failed the accounting final that year, you organized that emergency trip to Bal Harbor for retail therapy."

"The koi ponds are very rejuvenating," I say evenly.

"You look like you're in mourning." Ruby nudges my shoulder.

I glance down at my blue dress. "This is Balenciaga."

The wind blows a piece of hair across my face, and I tuck it back behind my ear as my phone vibrates.

Vivaro has totally ghosted me. I took down the collaboration posts I made well in advance of the post I put up this morning of Ruby and me getting off the plane at LAX.

It has a hundred comments, but I'm looking at one in particular.

Miles left three blue hearts on it.

"What?" Ruby asks. "You thought you could walk away and Miles wouldn't care?"

Nova cocks her head.

"I didn't walk away," I say.

"You moved out," Nova clarifies.

"Yes. The Kodiaks are in the middle of a season, and Miles is on the verge of everything he wants." I swallow the emotion that rises. "It's messy. Everyone thinks I'm the problem because it's happened since me."

"So?"

"Well... technically, they're right. Miles needs to focus on himself. At least for now."

I turn the phone over in my hand, fantasizing about tossing it into the ocean.

Except that he got it for me. And even if I did throw it, I have two more that he bought me—in different colors.

Damn. Even when I try not to think about him, he's right there.

"For the record, I want what's best for you but I'm not sure I support this," Ruby says.

"You're going to just back off until the end of the season?" Nova adds.

I start to type out a message but delete it because that will give Miles an opening.

If there's one thing he's good at, it's playing the long game.

So am I.

"Is that a piece of Elise's line?" I ask Nova as she changes into a cute shift dress in the hotel suite she, Ruby, and I are sharing. Her hair falls in waves around her shoulders across the cream fabric.

"Her clothes are beautiful," my friend gushes. "I bought some after your sorority retreat, but I wish they came in brighter colors." She twists a piece of the blond-and-pink hair that's been a mainstay for as long as I've known her.

"Not everyone is as genius with color as you."

Nova and I are visiting the Coastal Gallery to persuade them of hosting a solo show. Even though my friend is already becoming an established name, this would be a massive profile boost—particularly since most of her shows to date have been on the East Coast.

"Thanks for making time for this," Nova says. "I couldn't do it without my right-hand woman by my side."

My friend is a bright spot in all the chaos. She's been paying me to help with her brand and social media, and asked if I would help her field new opportunities, too.

I vow to give her my best effort despite feeling as if my life is spiraling out of control.

"Go crush it," Ruby tells us when we head for the door. "I'll be by the pool when you're done."

I jump in the driver's seat of our rented Mustang, cranking the top down so the breeze flies through. The wind tickles my fingers, and I resist the urge to shut my eyes.

Finding parking is its own miracle, but in half an hour, Nova and I are walking into a long, low building in Santa Monica. The owner introduces himself, shaking both our hands.

"This is Brooke. She handles my PR," says Nova.

I blink at the intro. Though I've been helping with her social and strategy for a couple of months now, I can't help but think that this feels like her offering me, *giving* me, a promotion.

More than that, she's putting her trust in me.

My chest tightens.

He walks us around, then takes us to a meeting room in the back lined with windows. We sit around a huge glass table along with a gallery assistant who's taking notes.

"We'd love to showcase some of your existing work."

"I was hoping to feature new pieces." Nova pulls out the portfolio at her side and lays out some of them.

His expression falls. "Our audience would respond best to the work you're known for."

"You must appreciate what it's like to want to go in a different direction." I smile at him. "I mean, you said yourself you retired from corporate life to do this."

He nods thoughtfully. "But we already have an abstract exhibit scheduled for next year."

I want to be strong for her, and I'm not letting some guy push my friend around, professionally or otherwise.

"Then maybe this isn't the right time," I say.

Nova glances at me but doesn't say anything.

After a bit more conversation and some polite exchanges, my friend and I step out into the main gallery space.

"They're a big deal, but you can't go in and bend

to everything they ask. He has to respect you," I say under my breath.

She doesn't look convinced.

"But if you want to go with it..." I go on.

"No. I trust you."

I nod, the blood pounding in my veins feeling like confidence. "Good."

13

———

MILES

When I was a kid, I used to love going to fairs—the rides, the games, the music. They've all gotten bigger since I was young. Case in point: the new amusement park opening near Fort Collins this weekend.

Someone on their PR team reached out to see if I would help them open it. Now, I'm in the front seat of a roller coaster car, sitting next to a photographer filming it all.

"I'm surprised your girlfriend didn't want to come," the woman calls over the wind as the car climbs higher. "She afraid of heights?"

I smile, but it's tight. "She's not afraid of anything."

Including walking away from me.

The thought sneaks in before I can stop it. The

memory of watching her walk out the door plays on repeat every time I close my eyes. It's the worst gut punch I've ever experienced.

We're not broken up. It's space.

I tell myself for the hundredth time.

Thing is, I've never had a woman say that to me before and never been close enough that I would've had to analyze what the hell that even meant.

When you try not to spend every second thinking about the person you've been spending every second thinking about, you need to replace them with some-thing else.

Distraction is something I'm an expert at.

Hence, amusement park.

The roller coaster car reaches the peak and drops.

Screams go up.

Human beings built these rolling metal monsters to see how much we can feel. By the second loop, I'm feeling way too much.

The rest of the ride, I'm preoccupied, right up until I'm stepping off at the end and my phone rings.

"Drug test came back." My agent's voice comes over the phone as I head toward the sponsor's booth to take more photos. "It's clean."

My eyes close in relief. Even though I knew I did nothing wrong, part of me was on edge until we got the official results. "So, the five-game suspension's going to lift? I can get back in uniform what, tomorrow?"

"I'm working on that."

There's a line of fans almost as long as the ride for the coaster.

Brooke doesn't want to be around me, but that doesn't mean other people don't. The thought is shitty, but a small, petty part of me feels good thinking it.

A bigger part of me feels like it's been stomped into a paste using stiletto heels. Guess that's the difference in being sore over someone you liked and having your heart ripped out and handed to you.

"The season isn't over. Go to the gym. Keep your head down. We need to focus." My agent's voice brings me back.

"That's what I'm doing." My hand covers my mouth. "Excuse me."

I step behind the building and throw up next to a plant.

BROOKE

"Brooke, are you coming down for dinner?" Mom's voice echoes up the stairs.

I haven't lived with my parents since before college. My room is still perfectly preserved, which I should be grateful for, but it brings back too many memories.

I start to say no, but my stomach growls. When was the last time I ate anything? I honestly can't remember.

Since I moved back in a week ago, I've been trying to keep my distance from Miles, but I can't help wondering what he's doing practically every second.

I click over to Miles's profile on social media. I don't expect to see any updates. He's on suspension, for goodness' sake.

What's there has my brows shooting up.

He went to the opening of a new amusement park. There's a woman hanging off him. Commenters are saying how cute they look.

It's not as though I wanted him lying on his couch devastated. If getting out is helping him feel better, then I'm relieved, but I'm not sure an amusement park outing is what he needs right now.

Maybe I made the wrong choice by putting space between us. This relationship is new. What if we're not close enough to handle this?

The text comes in while I'm still thinking of him.

Miles: Drug test came back clean.

My heart lifts. Hell yes. I do a fist pump in the air because no one's watching but it still feels good.

Brooke: I'm glad.

Miles: Thanks, Princess. Me too.

So, if the drugs weren't Miles's, which I knew for myself even if others didn't, whose were they?

I've been turning over the possibilities in my mind.

Miles is beloved in the league and in this city. The Kodiaks, on the other hand, have a bullseye on their backs.

What if the accident in Vegas gave someone the idea to target him?

"Brooke?!" My mom's voice is louder this time.

I shove the phone in my pocket and head to the dining room where my parents are already seated, plus my brother.

"Wow. Big happy family," I observe.

My mom and dad have the TV on, which features soundless commentary of my mom's campaign, then they do a split screen with a video of Miles and me at the all-star game.

I flinch. "What is that?"

Mom clicks off the TV. "The news cycle. Someone always finds something to pick at. We'll make it through. Ellis women, after all. We don't give up without a fight."

I'm grateful for her saying it.

"How was your game?" Dad's the one to ask Jay, not me.

"It was okay."

"You lost by twenty, got your asses handed to you," I observe, earning a dirty look. "Good thing Miles is back in two more games. Is there any word on what happened?"

"Nothing official."

"Right. Because that's why I'm asking my brother on the team instead of reading the news."

Jay rolls his eyes.

"No more talk about basketball," Mom decides.

I shift in my seat. "Oh good. Let's talk politics."

"Kevin's family is making progress on their merger. It will become one of the largest firms in the state."

"So sorry I couldn't marry into them," I say under my breath.

"Our image could use the polishing. They're up for an ethics award."

I throw my napkin on the table. The idea of Kevin claiming the moral high ground in any sense is laughable. "Excuse me. I can't eat right now."

I THROW myself into drafting some social media content for Nova. I love her new direction and approach. It's hard to be a creator, an artist, and follow a new path—especially when her career relies on being able to bring her fans along with her.

After our visit to LA, I followed up with the owner at the Coastal Gallery. He still isn't convinced of Nova's new direction, but I've been working to remind him how brilliant and in-demand she is through a series of posts highlighting her recent successes. They've liked more than one of the posts, so I know they're seeing them.

I'm nearly ready to send him a draft pitch. Nova will curate a completely original collection of paintings in a fresh new style. And after all, isn't that what his patrons want? For Coastal to be a trailblazer? All he has to do is say yes.

Remembering my talk with Elise in New York, I sent an email to Sarah to ask for any help with partnerships and included my contact info. She said she'd get back to me shortly.

My mind keeps wandering.

I go to the suitcase I half unpacked and pull out the glittery red heels that Miles had fixed for me after the costume party.

I step into them. They look ridiculous with my outfit, but I don't take them off as I click around my room because they make me think of the party. Me asking him to go to the Kappa retreat with me.

God, I was naive. Had no clue how hard I would fall.

I can't resist typing out a text.

Brooke: When are you playing next?

I drop into the chair in front of my desk to work for a minute, two, before my phone buzzes.

Miles: Still waiting to hear back from my agent.

Brooke: Guess you can celebrate on roller coasters with Kodashians in the meantime.

Miles: Hah. Funny thing, there's only one girl I want to be with.

Longing sneaks up, making my next breath painful.

I've always wanted to be my own person, and I am. But it feels as if when I walked out with that suitcase, he kept part of me.

I cross my legs and my shoes sparkle red in the light.

"There's no place like home." The words from the Wizard of Oz come back to me.

I'm in the house I grew up in with my family, but it feels as if my home is somewhere else entirely.

My finger finds the call button before I can stop myself.

"Hey." Miles's voice is surprised and pleased.

"Hey."

If he's upset that I called, there's no trace of it in his tone, which only makes me want to crawl through the phone and into his arms.

The fact that he answered after one ring makes me think he might let me.

"How's the space going?" he asks.

He's right. This was probably a bad idea. "If you don't want to talk—"

"Not what I meant. I'm glad you called."

The knot in my chest loosens. "How's life?"

He sighs. "You want the truth?"

"No. Lie to me."

There's a low chuckle. "Well, the team is doing amazing. We're in first, and I got a triple-double tonight."

"Mmm." The sound of his voice is lifting my spirits already. "What else?"

"Waffles learned to cook. He made a killer soufflé this morning."

I laugh, unable to help picturing it.

"And... I'm talking to my favorite person. How about you?"

I bite my cheek, channeling my creativity to make up the best case scenario. "Well, Nova just sold three pieces in her new style. I stumbled on a massive designer trunk sale and bought one of everything at seventy percent off. Plus, Kevin's family firm is definitely not winning an award for ethics."

There's silence on the line.

"I killed the vibe," I say, apologetic.

"Don't worry about it."

I rub my tired face as I drop onto the bed. One of my shoes slips off my foot and clatters to the floor.

"What was that?" he asks.

I wince. "My shoe."

"The red ones? I was bummed you'd taken them. I guess I hoped you'd leave them here. For the memories."

The fact that he noticed makes my chest twinge. "That's why I wanted them with me."

He pauses. "Is it helping? The space?"

My eyes burn at the backs and I take a deep breath.

"Yeah." I'm not sure.

"Listen. I wanted to tell you that I did try coke once. It was a rough spot and I went to this party. My parents were fighting after the split, and my Grams was having financial problems. I was at risk of getting cut from my team as a senior, which would mean no college scholarship and no pro ball. It was stupid. I was stupid."

I swallow. "I thought you would have told me. Not because it changes how I think of you, but because of the accusations back in college when the Kappas found Kevin's drugs in my room."

"I think that's partly why I didn't. I don't want to make your life harder. But recently I've realized you're not the only one trying to look a certain way. I want to be the fun guy. The popular guy. Not the doubting one. Not the desperate one." He takes a breath. "The only reason Jay knew is that he was there for the aftermath. He made sure I didn't entertain it again."

For a moment, I'm grateful to my brother for taking care of Miles and being a good friend.

"You can show me all the versions of you," I promise. "It won't scare me away."

He exhales softly.

A text pings my phone.

Unknown: Hey Brooke, it's Sarah from Elise's team. Just emailed you some examples.

"I should go," I say, reluctant. If I don't hang up now, I might keep talking to him all night. So much for giving us both some space.

"Sure." He sounds every bit as unsatisfied. "Night, Princess. I'll call you tomorrow?"

My lips twitch. "Is that how it works?"

"You don't want to talk tomorrow, then don't answer." He pauses. "You're totally going to answer."

The smile in his tone warms me.

When we click off, I feel better than before.

Sarah: Between you and me, I wish she'd picked you for the deal.

Brooke: You're sweet.

Sarah: If it helps, I don't think Caroline's engagement swayed her. Elise never liked Kevin. I remember hearing rumors about him being

involved in some shady stuff. Nothing concrete, but whispers. I never knew what to believe.

Despite his apology, which seemed sincere, I'm curious.

I should let it go, thank her for the support and get back to work.

What I say instead is:

Do you remember any specific incidents?

It's none of my business. She has every right to tell me that, and if I were smart, I'd say it to myself too.

I'm about to sign off when dots appear.

Sarah: He was involved in this top-secret cheating ring back in law school.

I blink at my phone. That's not what I was expecting.

Not at all.

14

MILES

"I don't want to bankrupt you."

I blink at my grams. "Hmm?"

She nods to Illinois Avenue and the shiny new hotel on it. "You can't afford this."

We're sitting around the coffee table in the lounge, the space cheerfully illuminated with bright light streaming in the windows. The game is spread out in front of us, a new edition that makes it easy to transport without having to put everything back in the box.

"Sure I can." I peel bills off my stack and pass them over to her.

In the past month, Grams's arm has healed well, and the staff have been attentive and kept me updated on any changes in her health.

A TV flashes on one wall, silent with subtitles.

A few residents enter the room, and my grandmother waves.

"Glad you're making friends," I say as they whisper to one another.

"I've tried watching the sports news, but it's a lot of men with strong opinions," Grams says. "But I couldn't help but see what's happened. And my neighbors are asking."

About me, she means.

"I'm sorry people are asking." It didn't occur to me that she'd bear the brunt of any gossip.

Not unlike how Brooke has been.

"I don't care what anyone thinks. I care about you." She straightens, eyes blue and sharp.

The past week flashes through my mind.

"Nothing happened." I need her to believe me. More than I need any other person to.

She nods slowly. "We all have lessons to learn, particularly when we're young."

It twists my gut that she's questioning me.

"It was a mistake." I force a smile. "A misunderstanding."

"Misunderstandings are the most dangerous because we assume everyone sees things our way. They have a habit of escalating. I don't want you to forget where you came from. Or what kind of man you are."

Miles: You guys ready for the game tonight?

Miles: Dallas has been leaking oil in the fourth. Punish them for it.

Rookie: Thanks, man. Can't wait to have you back.

Damon: Glad the drug test came back clean.

Damon: Not that we weren't sure.

Jay: We'll take care of Dallas. You take care of you.

I SLOUCH on the couch as I watch the Kodiaks struggle through the third game without me.

It's painful to see my team fumbling, knowing I should be out there.

I invited Rookie to come with me to the amusement park the other day, but he passed, saying he had another commitment. Jay's answering in polite monosyllables since Brooke walked out.

Everything sucks.

Waffles senses my frustration and shifts into my lap, his tongue lolling out as he nuzzles against my stomach.

"At least you're here for me, buddy." I scratch behind his ears.

My thoughts drift to Brooke.

I miss her smile, her laugh, the way she fits perfectly in my arms. I hate that I can't be there for her right now, that I can't hold her and tell her everything's going to be okay.

The ache in my chest grows, and I go to the kitchen and open the stainless fridge. Beer stares me down.

I grab a soda and slam the door.

The buzzing of my phone interrupts my brooding.

My agent. I hit Accept and greet him brusquely.

"Miles. Bad news. Suspension stands," he says evenly.

"What? Why?"

He drones on about procedures and the ongoing inquiry, but I tune it out before hanging up.

I'm sitting all five games, for no reason.

When I click off, I see a text from an old friend inviting me to a party.

Dante and I used to play in college, though he didn't go on to get drafted. He's in town for the weekend, saying he's had a rough time and would love it if I came.

I hesitate, glancing at the TV just in time to see

the Kodiaks miss another easy shot. I make a split-second decision.

"I'm going out."

I leave Waffles, promising to be back soon.

When I arrive, the party is in full swing, the bass thumping through the walls.

"You need a drink!" Dante offers me a beer in the kitchen.

"Nah, I'm good."

"Come on. It's been a rough week and I need a buddy." He clocks my reluctance. "I'll give you all the dirt on Hawkins," he says, a slow grin creeping across his face. "He was on my high school team."

Well, fuck. This could be a chance for me to get insight into our biggest competition.

It's a worthy cause.

So, I accept the beer he hands me.

He tells me more about Hawkins's reputation, that in high school he not only engaged in a ton of trash talk, but more than once suggested playing dirtier. That before finals, tried to break up the other team's captain and his girlfriend.

I file that away as I find myself drinking more and more. It's less about keeping pace with him and keeping him talking, and more trying to dull the ache of being separated from my team and Brooke.

Conversations swirl around me, but I barely register the words.

I see the final score on a TV out of the corner of my eye. Guilt settles into my gut.

Go to the gym. Keep your head down.

My agent's words come back to me.

I slam my empty cup on the table and stumble outside, the cool night air hitting me like a slap in the face. In my drunken haze, an idea takes hold.

Calling a limo is easy.

I stop at my place to get Waffles, chuckling as he licks my face excitedly. "We're going on an adventure, buddy."

I tuck him under my arm and head for the arena's side door.

I navigate the dark hallways, memories of better times flooding back. Waffles trots ahead, his tail wagging as he explores this new playground. His enthusiasm is contagious, and I find myself grinning despite the heaviness in my chest.

After swiping into another two security zones, we end up in the locker room, and I sink onto the bench in front of my locker. Waffles hops up beside me, his warm body pressed against my thigh.

"What are we going to do, Waffles?" I whisper, burying my face in his soft fur.

Waffles cocks his head, his ears perked up. For a

moment, I swear he understands every word. I lean back, my head spinning with anger.

But then Brooke's face flashes through my mind, her eyes filled with disappointment and hurt. She wouldn't want this. She wouldn't want me to throw away everything we've fought for, everything we have.

I run a hand over my locker. For the first time since everything happened, it strikes me that someone was in here.

Getting in here requires ID. There's no way someone wandered in here and left drugs in my locker by mistake.

And I saw the faces of every guy on my parade out of here. None of them did this.

So, who did?

I don't hear the footsteps approaching until it's too late.

"Hey! What are you doing in here?" a gruff voice demands.

I jump to my feet, swaying. Waffles barks, his tail wagging as he bounds over to the security guard. The guard's stern expression softens slightly as Waffles sniffs his shoes, his tongue lolling out in a goofy grin.

"It's me. Miles Garrett." My brain struggles to form a coherent excuse.

The guard's eyes narrow with uncertainty. "You're not supposed to be in here given your probation."

"I'm working out. Got to get back into game shape." I flash a grin.

He reaches for his radio.

I take a stumbling step forward. "No. Come on, man."

But it's too late. The guard is already speaking into his radio. Waffles, oblivious to the seriousness of the situation, trots back to me, tail wagging happily.

I sink back onto the bench, my head in my hands. I'm supposed to be proving my innocence, not getting into more trouble. Brooke's going to be so disappointed in me. So is Grams.

Two more security guys emerge from the hallway, their expressions solemn.

Not good.

I pull Waffles back into my arms. He licks my chin.

"I screwed up, buddy," I whisper. "But I'm going to fix it."

15

MILES

Jay: We need to talk. The entire team.

Jay: Today.

Miles: I'm there.

"This is a secret meeting. Anyone asks, it never happened." Jay looks around the circle of guys in the back room at Mile High.

"Wait." Damon holds up a hand. "First we have to sign in blood."

Rookie rolls up a sleeve, and Clay shoots him a look.

"It was a joke," Clay says.

"It was?" Atlas frowns.

I clear my throat, and every set of eyes slides to me.

"Listen, I know I'm scheduled to be back in practice in a few days. I started a little early."

"You got drunk and broke into the gym," Clay corrects.

I called this meeting because, aside from my suspension, there's the very real issue that half the guys on the team don't believe the drugs in my locker weren't mine.

I hold up a hand. "I wanted to make sure I didn't lose conditioning."

Rookie snorts, but Clay doesn't blink.

Joking around isn't going to fix this. I've got the message.

"Fine. I missed it. I missed you guys." I rub a hand over my neck. "The team has always been important to me, but I didn't see how important until we were in this position. I didn't care about winning as much as some of you, but what mattered was the fact that we were in it together. Lately, it's felt like we're not together."

"The team's struggling, and it's showing up on the court," Jay says. "Everyone's gotten stronger after the trade deadline, but instead of improving, we're down a shooting guard and dealing with a shitstorm."

I rise, pacing the room. "You know I like to joke

around, but I want this as much as any of you. If you think I took a bump after the all-star game, raise a hand."

A couple of arms rise slowly.

"You think I risked this team by leaving drugs in my own fucking locker at the Kodiaks' arena, raise a hand," I say.

The hands lower.

"When you put it that way," Atlas starts.

"But what's the alternative?" Rookie demands.

Grim faces around the circle exchange looks.

"Someone's targeting the team." We turn toward the door where Chloe leans against the frame.

"The fuck is she doing here?" Atlas grumbles.

"I asked her to come."

Jay's admission has my brows lifting.

"Should we wait on Harlan too? James?" Clay asks deadpan.

Jay ignores him. "As the team captain, I want every guy in here to swear you had nothing to do with this."

One by one, they do.

"Good. So, it wasn't one of us. Who's left?"

Chloe folds her arms. "I spoke to security. They showed me tapes. There was no one unusual there that night."

"Which means it must have been staff," Jay says.

Unease ripples through the room.

"There are a couple hundred people in the organization," Chloe says.

"But how many have access to the locker room?" Rookie asks.

Chloe and Jay exchange a look.

"Thirty," Chloe says. It sounds like a guess.

"Hard to imagine someone has a hate-on for Miles. So, it's probably money. Someone who wants us to go down."

Clay grunts. "Boston. What if Hawkins decided talking wasn't enough?"

That's a shitty thought, but he's not wrong.

"Guy's been known to skirt the rules," Jay says slowly.

"We know he's no Kodiaks fan," Damon adds.

My mind is trying to piece it together. I see the conversation with Dante the other night in a new light.

"Hell, he was in Vegas, too." I was talking to him before my drink got spiked.

We all sit with that a minute.

"What do we do?" Rookie asks.

"Nothing," Jay says firmly. "Keep your noses clean. Focus on the season. Get back into winning form."

"Can we tell the media someone is behind this?" Atlas suggests.

Chloe shakes her head. "They won't believe it. It will sound like we're deflecting instead of handling our problems internally."

No one likes that, but there's not much we can do about it.

"I'll talk to Harlan about increasing security," Chloe says.

We all nod.

"Kodiaks on three," Jay calls.

We put our hands in.

"Catch you at practice," Rookie says, clapping me on the shoulder.

"Thanks, man."

Chloe and the guys disperse one by one, leaving Jay and me. The room feels empty even though it's not that big.

"Vacation's almost over." Jay lingers by the door as I grab my things.

"Thank fuck. Don't know what to do with myself all week. Lying on the couch staring at the ceiling and watching *The Bachelor* doesn't help."

My friend shakes his head.

I hesitate before asking, "How's Brooke?"

"You guys don't talk?"

"It's not the same." Confessing to my best friend about his sister feels awkward, and from the look on his face, he's right there with me.

"I get why she wanted a break. I made life extra rough for her, and maybe I fell harder than she did," I admit.

"That's not it." Jay frowns, rubbing a hand over his face. "She's been through some things. Kevin treated her like shit, then her sorority sisters turned their backs on her too? You might think I don't want to see you guys together, but it's not because she's my sister. It's because the attention'll be even worse this time around with her being linked to you. After what we grew up with and Mom's career, I don't want that for her."

"I can protect her."

"Not from all of it, you can't. You can't be there all the time."

"Then I'll be there after," I say firmly. "This time. Every time."

Jay grunts, as if my commitment made this worse.

"What?" I challenge.

"I think that was her excuse for leaving, and as far as I'm concerned, it's more than enough. But if I know my sister, she half believes what they're saying. That she's bad for you."

Disbelief rises up. "That's bullshit. We both know it."

He stares me down. "Maybe you should tell her."

BROOKE

Dear Nova and Brooke,

We enjoyed meeting you in person and appreciated you sending a draft partnership agreement. Please find it attached with minor revisions. We look forward to hosting you this April and exposing your work to our community.

Sincerely,
The Coastal Gallery Team

"Six. No, seven." I count off the pieces for the show.

"What's wrong?" Nova asks.

"This piece." I hold up a photo on my phone. "You were going to send it to Coastal for the show."

After getting the email yesterday, we did a happy

dance and celebrated before filling out the paperwork.

They insisted on a mix of old and new pieces, including a couple of specific floral paintings Nova finished last year. So, we confirmed and Nova added in the list of pieces she would send the gallery, then signed.

Today, we're organizing the art, working off that list.

We go through cartons, and I open the containers one after the other.

"Well, shit." Nova looks around the exposed art, dissatisfied.

"Did you send it to New York for another exhibition?" I ask her.

"Maybe? That piece was the one Coastal was most excited about." She chews her lip.

I'm unwilling to let anything bring us down after we got the agreement signed. It was a huge win. Anything else is fixable.

"We'll be honest," I suggest. "Tell him we planned on having it available but it's not."

"You don't think he'll hate it? It is in the contract we sent back," she reminds me.

"No way. He loves your work. We'll send him photos of a three new pieces and he can take his pick," I suggest. "Your latest paintings are amazing."

"I appreciate you saying that. Not all the reactions have been positive."

Her gaze drops to her phone on the table, and I know what she's thinking.

Her posts featuring new art have less engagement, and half the comments on them are asking when she'll make more dancers or floral art.

"Ignore the comments. I will respond for you," I say.

Nova blows out a breath. "You're the best. Really."

A notification on her phone interrupts us. My friend glances at the screen.

"Shoot. I told Clay I'd meet him," she says, clicking off her phone.

I push off the wall and walk over to her, then place my hands on her shoulders. "Go meet your husband. I'll take another look around and if I can't find the piece, I'll photograph your available new ones and send them to him for his choice."

"Okay. But please don't stay too late. Call me if you need anything."

We hug, and I watch as she leaves.

"All right, flower painting. Where the hell are you?" I plant my hands on my hips and scan the room.

Some time later, my phone rings. *Miles.*

"Hey," I answer, my heart skipping.

"Hi. What's up?"

It's so good hearing his voice. It feels like things are normal with us, even if they aren't.

"Helping Nova get ready for this show. But I sent her home to be with Clay."

I fill him in.

"Wow. That gallery sounds like the real deal. Way to go."

"Thanks." My lips twitch. "Except for the whole missing piece thing. I'm going to send him some new options and everything will be fine. You're playing tomorrow?"

"Uh-huh. Had a meeting with the guys to get on the same page."

"I'm glad."

He pauses. "Jay said something to me."

"Oh no." I start pacing the room.

"He wants me to stop hurting his sister."

My toe catches on a box and I narrowly avoid going sprawling across the floor. "You're not hurting me," I say.

"Yeah, I am. I hurt your reputation. I made you worry. All I want to do is make your life better, Princess, and I couldn't."

My chest aches. "That's not true."

"I'm going to fix it. Starting now. Did you eat?"

"Eat?" I echo. "Dinner or lunch?"

"I'll take that as a no. When was the last time you were outside? It's a beautiful Wednesday."

"It's Wednesday?" I wince.

"What you need is a walk and a picnic."

Longing tugs at me. Both sounds great.

"I can't," I say reluctantly. "I need to finish this."

We hang up so I can get back to work.

Half an hour later, there's a knock at the door. I rise to get it, finding Miles on the other side.

He's holding a tree in one hand and a huge brown paper bag from my favorite takeout place in the other but it's the huge grin on his face that makes me feel the more renewed.

"I couldn't get you outside for a picnic," he says sheepishly, "so I brought outside to you."

MILES HOLDS out the package of rolls to me and I take one. I'm sitting on the blanket he spread across the floor, and when I bite into the roll, I can't help but groan in appreciation. "So good. Missed this."

"Fresh rolls?"

"Eating with you." The words slip out before I can stop them.

A slow grin spreads across his face. "What else did you miss?"

"Your coffee. My parents have a perfectly good Nespresso, but it's not the same." It really isn't. Nothing at home compares to mornings in his kitchen.

"Snob."

I shrug and reach for my drink, letting more truth spill out. "I miss Waffles."

"He misses you."

"I miss your bathtub. I had the best bubble baths in there." The memory warms my cheeks.

"Mmm. Including the one where you took that picture and sent it to me on the road." He shakes his head.

I laugh, remembering. "Oh my God. I forgot that."

"It wasn't an accident," he says with certainty.

"It was completely an accident."

We're both grinning now.

My breath catches as he brushes a piece of hair from my face.

"Ninety-four," he murmurs.

"Ninety-four what?"

"That's how many nights I was on the road last year. I had to spend that many nights without you. I don't want to spend any more."

My smile fades as I search his face, my heart picking up speed.

He moves closer, and his next words make my chest tight. "I know you're used to being attacked, to people not having your back, but I've got you. The pressure on me is new, but I can take it because I've seen what you deal with. If life is hard right now, I'd still rather go through it with you."

My throat constricts as he continues. "If people think you're making my life worse, they can fuck off. All the way off. Because they don't know me, and if they did, they'd know my life has only been better with you in it. You make me a better basketball player. A better teammate. A better man."

The intensity in his eyes makes my heart race.

"I miss you as my friend," he goes on. "I miss you next to me. I miss hearing you laugh. I miss you as a person, but most of all, I miss you as the person who makes me feel like I'm so damn lucky to be me."

Everything in me aches to believe him as he whispers, "I can't promise every minute will be perfect, but it'll be more perfect because we'll have each other. We're better together, Brooke. I know you see it. I want to give us another chance, and I don't want to wait until the end of the season to do it."

I can't speak. His phone is peeking out of his pocket and the screen lights up, showing a photo of us from before the sorority retreat—on of the ones Nova took on the rooftop when we were pretending.

I look up at him. "You still have that as your home screen?"

His lips twitch. "It was the first time I got to look at you like you were mine."

The last of my resistance crumbles. I rise up onto my knees and kiss him.

16

BROOKE

Miles's hands are already on me.

The urgency in his touch sends a thrill through me. I wrap my arms around his neck, pulling him closer as our kiss deepens. I feel as if I've been waiting for this moment for years—to be in Miles's arms again, to feel his lips on mine, to know that he's here and he's not going anywhere.

The light spills in the front windows, and I tug him toward the office in the back to block us from view. We stumble our way there, our lips never breaking contact, and I can't help but feel a sense of rightness.

This is where I belong, in Miles's arms. No matter what happens with our lives, I know that I can always come back to this.

I kick off my shoes, leaving a trail of clothing down the hall.

Once we reach the office, Miles pulls back for a moment, his eyes searching mine. The only lighting is what spills through from the other room, casting shadows on the walls as our bodies move closer. I see the hunger in Miles's eyes as my vision adjusts, the way his muscles tense with each touch.

"Are you sure about this?" he asks, his voice husky with desire.

I nod, my heart pounding. The scent of Miles's cologne mixes with the warmth of our bodies. It fills my senses and makes my heart race even faster. "I've never been more sure of anything."

With that, he kisses me again, his hands roaming my body. As our kisses deepen, I taste the sweetness of his lips, a familiar and comforting taste that has always been uniquely his.

I reach for the hem of his shirt, pulling it over his head and discarding it on the floor. His skin is warm beneath my fingertips, and I revel in the solid strength of his muscles. Our bodies fit together like pieces of a puzzle, each touch sparking a symphony of sensations that resonates deep within me.

My skin tingles under Miles's touch, every nerve alive and craving his hands on me. His fingertips trace paths along my body, igniting sparks of pleasure with each caress. I run my hands over his broad shoulders and down his back, feeling the warmth of his skin and the strength of his embrace.

Our breaths come in ragged gasps, mingling together in the quiet of the room. The only other sounds are the occasional creak of the desk beneath us and the soft moans and whimpers that escape our lips.

My heart races as Miles's lips trail down my neck, sending shivers of desire through me. The world outside our little bubble fades away, leaving only the two of us in this moment. His hands move with purpose and passion, each touch igniting a fire within me that threatens to consume us both.

He skims his hands down my waist, over my ass. He unzips my jeans, drags them over my hips, and my thong with them. Miles's gaze travels down my body, his eyes dark with desire. I feel a rush of heat at his intensity, at the hunger in his eyes that matches my own. His hands trace the curves of my body with reverence, as if committing every inch to memory.

His mouth finds mine again, a searing kiss that leaves me breathless. I melt into him, lost in the heady whirlwind of passion that swirls between us.

His touch strokes lower, between my thighs. My breath hitches. My body is responding to his touch, obeying the primal desire that courses through me.

"Miles," I murmur, my voice barely audible, "I've missed this."

His eyes lock with mine, his face a mix of longing and desire. "I've missed you, Princess."

There's a table with packing supplies in the corner, and he sweeps it to clear it. He lifts me up onto it and follows me down, each touch sending a ripple of pleasure through me. Miles's eyes never leave mine, his face a canvas of raw emotion.

His fingers trace delicate paths along my skin, every touch a reminder of the trust we've shared. I arch my back, my fingers searching out the edge of the table as our embrace deepens. Miles's lips find my neck, his breath hot and heavy against my skin. I close my eyes, savoring the feeling of his touch, the warmth of his body pressed against mine.

As he continues his exploration, it's just us alone in our own little universe, where nothing matters but the feeling of his touch, the heat of his passion, the sound of our breaths.

"I need you," I whisper, my voice barely above a whisper.

He looks down at me, his eyes dark with desire, his face a testament to the intensity of our connection. He nods, his hands trembling slightly as he reaches for me.

He positions himself between my legs, his gaze

never leaving mine. I can feel the tension in his body, the intensity of his desire mirrored in every muscle, every movement. With a grace that belies his strength, he enters me, our bodies becoming one in a union that feels as natural and right as the world around us.

I gasp at the feeling of his warmth, his body pressing against me, his hips moving in a rhythm that matches the pounding of my heart. Our eyes lock, a silent communication of love and desire that transcends words. I can see his hunger, his longing, his unwavering commitment to me.

I wrap my arms around him, pulling him closer, my body arching to meet his every thrust. Every touch, every movement, is another reminder of the connection that has always existed between us. A bond that has been tested but never broken.

As our bodies move together, our breaths sync, our hearts beating in time with each other. It's a dance we've done a thousand times, but this time feels different, more powerful, more intimate. The pleasure builds, a wave of sensation that threatens to consume me.

"Brooke," Miles breathes, his voice a low growl. His hands grip my hips, his eyes never leaving mine. "I'm close."

A shiver runs down my spine, the anticipation

heightening my senses. I meet his gaze, a challenge in my eyes. "Me too."

He kisses me hard, our breaths matching in a wild cadence. Each movement of his hips sends a ripple of pleasure through me, the tension building until I can't take it anymore.

"Miles," I whimper, arching my back. "Now."

He nods, his breath hot on my neck. His movements become more frenzied, his body pressing against mine. Miles's hair is tousled, his skin flushed and glistening with sweat as he moves above me. His eyes are intense and focused, locked on mine.

"Brooke," he groans, his voice hoarse.

"With you," I gasp, my body trembling.

Miles's chest rises and falls rapidly, beads of sweat forming on his brow as he looks into my eyes, every muscle tense and poised. Our bodies writhe and tremble as the pleasure consumes us, leaving us gasping and spent in its wake.

As our breaths slowly return to normal, I cling to Miles, savoring the feeling of his warmth, his strength.

"Two seventy-one," I murmur.

"Hmm?"

"That's how many nights you'll have left after traveling."

He pulls me closer, a small smile playing on his lips. "I want to spend them all with you."

17

MILES

HOOPSNEWS UPDATE: 7TH RANKED KODIAKS FACE 8TH-RANKED OKC WITH GARRETT BACK IN THE LINEUP

The locker room buzzes with energy as I go through my pregame routine.

It's my first time back on the court with the Kodiaks since the suspension. The weight of the upcoming game is heavy on my shoulders but fuck, does it feel good to be back.

Jay meticulously tapes his ankles. He looks up as I approach. "Ready for this?"

I nod and smile. "Hell yeah."

Since the suspension, Chloe's doing her best to

field media inquiries, but mostly it's people trying to stir up shit. Within a few more days, new storylines will emerge, and they'll move on.

Like I want to move on.

Even Hawkins doesn't have any fresh hot takes in the media this morning.

Rookie bounds over, his enthusiasm undiminished by the somber atmosphere. "It's good to have you back. We've missed you out there."

I clap him on the shoulder, grateful for his unwavering support.

Across the room, Clay grunts. "We can't afford any more distractions."

I bristle at his words, but before I can respond, Coach calls us in for a final huddle.

"Listen up, everyone. This game is critical. We're fighting for our playoff spot, and every possession counts."

As we take the court for warmups, I scan the stands. Brooke couldn't come tonight because of a commitment for Nova. She said she'd reschedule, but I told her not to worry about it.

Now, I wish to hell she was here.

The game against OKC is a grind from the opening tip-off. My shots are off, my passes erratic. I feel my teammates' frustration mounting with every missed opportunity, every defensive lapse. Jay barks orders, his tone sharp and unforgiving. Clay shakes his head in disgust as I botch a simple play. The scoreboard ticks away, the gap widening with each passing minute.

During a timeout, Coach pulls me aside. "What's going on out there? I need you to step up, to be the leader you have been—the one I know you can be."

I clench my jaw. "Yeah. You got it."

But the words feel hollow, the weight of my doubts echoing in my chest.

The final buzzer sounds, a devastating fifteen-point loss. The locker room is silent, the air heavy with disappointment and unspoken accusations.

I sit at my locker, my head in my hands, the walls closing in around me.

Jay approaches, his frustration palpable. "What happened out there? We needed you, and you disappeared on us."

I look up, meeting his gaze. "I couldn't find my rhythm. It won't happen again."

Rookie tries to interject, his voice filled with optimism. "Hey, it's one game. We'll bounce back."

Clay cuts him off. "Bounce back when? We're running out of time."

My fists clench with frustration, but he's not wrong.

Atlas raises a hand, silencing the room. "Enough talk. Miles is our brother. We stand with him."

The weight of their words settles on my shoulders as I head to media. But on my way, I spot a new face.

"Have we met?" I ask the cleaner who's sweeping up in the hallway. I make a point of knowing every person I see on a regular basis, especially the staff at the arena.

"No, I started this week. I'm George. Lisa just quit."

"Right." I shake his hand and file that away as I head to media, a spring in my step for the first time in weeks.

Because that sounds an awful lot like a clue.

BROOKE

"WE SHOULD TURN this over to the team," Miles says for the fifth time.

"Not without more information." I shift in the passenger seat.

After the game last night, Miles told me what he learned about the cleaner quitting.

Maybe she was involved.

"We're not private investigators, Princess. This is above my paygrade."

"No such thing." I wink at him. "Besides, you're more cut out for this than you thought. I'm impressed you got her contact information from HR."

"I can be charming, you know." Miles tosses me a cocky look, but there's no hiding the nerves underneath. His jaw is clenched, and his eyes are fixed on the road ahead.

"So. You going to move back in?" he asks casually.

"You want me to?"

Miles pretends to consider. "Would save me sending a stealth unit to your parents' house and removing all your belongings without you noticing."

My mouth falls open.

"I have a lot of belongings."

"All of them. Each shoe. Earring. Face cream thingy." He holds up fingers to count them off. "They're all coming back with me until you realize that's where you belong, too."

His words touch me. "I guess it would be less scandalous if I packed my own bags," I decide.

Miles grins, reaching out to take my hand in his. "Good. If there's anything we need to do differently this time around, I'm down to talk about it. Except for one thing."

"What's that?" Wariness rises up.

"I need you to be little spoon."

I turn to look out the window, my smile wide enough it hurts. "Okay."

As we pull into the parking lot, I take a deep breath, steeling myself for what's to come. I run through the scenarios in my head, imagining how the conversation might unfold. Will Lisa be willing to talk? Or will this be a dead end that leaves us right back where we started?

"You could stay in the car," Miles suggests.

"You think I'm going to scare her away? I'll have you know I can be very welcoming and approach-able. Kappa pledges were up twenty percent the year that I was recruitment chair."

"That's not it." Miles grunts. "I want to keep you as far away from this as possible."

My chest warms at his protective words. I shift closer, running my hands through his hair. "No way. We're in this together."

We enter the coffee shop, the bell above the door jingling softly. The air feels thick with anticipation as we take our seats, Miles's knee bouncing under the table. I give his hand a reassuring squeeze.

The bell above the door jingles again, and a middle-aged woman enters, her eyes darting around the room until they land on us. She recognizes

Miles right away, but she orders a drink and waits for it.

I stand and cross to her with a warm smile. "Hey, Lisa? Thank you for meeting with us."

I insist on buying her drink and she takes a seat, her hands wrapped tightly around her cup of coffee. "I'm not sure how much help I can be."

Miles leans in. "Someone planted drugs in my locker and tried to blame it on me. I need to find out who."

I squeeze Miles's arm, a warning. We can't scare her off before we've started.

My voice is gentle but firm. "Lisa, why did you quit your job with the team? It seems like a great place to work."

Lisa takes a deep breath, her eyes flickering between Miles and me. "I didn't want to get involved, but I saw something that didn't sit right with me."

Miles leans forward, and my fingers tighten on his arm.

Lisa continues, her voice growing stronger. "It was one of the training staff. They all have the same jackets. He seemed jumpy. He kept looking around as if he wasn't sure why he was there."

My heart races as I exchange a glance with Miles. This is the lead we've been hoping for.

Lisa's hands fidget with her cup. "I was cleaning

the locker room before the game, and I noticed him come in. He went straight to your locker, Miles."

Miles's jaw works.

I take a steadying breath, trying to keep my emotions in check. "Lisa, this is extremely important. Can you remember any other details about that night? Anything at all?"

Lisa furrows her brow, her eyes distant as she sifts through her memories. "I heard him talking on the phone on the way out, couldn't hear the other voice. He seemed agitated, like he was arguing with someone."

I nod, my mind racing. "Could you identify him?"

Lisa shakes her head. "I didn't get a good look and I don't know the coaching staff well. I remember thinking it was strange, but I didn't want to get involved. I should have come forward sooner."

Miles leans forward. "You're doing the right thing now. Thank you for being brave enough to tell us what you saw."

Lisa nods. I fix the smile on my face as the flicker of hope extinguishes in my chest.

There are no cameras in the locker rooms for privacy reasons, which means that it's one thing if she saw someone, but if she can't identify him, we're back to square one.

18

———

BROOKE

Nova: Need your help. It's a friend emergency.

The cryptic message came through after I got out of the shower. Miles was gone at practice, so I had the condo to myself.

As I pull up to Nova's house, I can't help but admire the beautiful exterior that she and Clay fell in love with months ago. I walk up to the front door and ring the doorbell.

Nova opens the door, her eyes wide and expression worried. "I'm so glad you're here." She pulls me into a warm hug before ushering me inside.

I step into the living room and pause. The furniture has been pushed to the center of the room.

"Was there an earthquake I didn't know about?" I ask.

"Close." Sierra is in the kitchen, pulling coffees and donuts out of a brown paper bag.

"Very funny." Nova stands amidst the chaos, her hands on her hips. "Clay's parents called, and they're coming to visit this weekend. You know his mom."

"She's that extra, huh?" Sierra asks.

"Her heart is in the right place."

"It's just made of ice," I add helpfully. "So that's the emergency?"

"Yes. I've been trying to rearrange this room for hours, but nothing seems to feel right." Frustration seeps into Nova's voice.

I set down my bag and take a closer look at the space. "Don't sweat it. A fresh perspective can make all the difference."

Nova's shoulders relax slightly. "I just want this house to feel like home. We've been here for months, but something's missing."

We move the furniture around, trying out different layouts.

I suggest moving the couch to the opposite wall, but Nova hesitates. "I'm not sure. I think it needs to face the fireplace."

After half an hour of pushing and pulling furniture around, it's not better.

"Carb break," Sierra suggests.

We pause and make our way to the kitchen. I pop a bite of sticky sweetness into my mouth.

"I haven't seen you guys in forever," Sierra gripes. "It's been a sausage fest at Mile High the past couple of weeks."

"No Kodashians?" I laugh.

She waves a hand. "They don't count."

"I'm sorry," Nova says. "I'm so preoccupied with this Coastal Gallery show." She fills Sierra in, finishing with how the gallery owner has very strong opinions on what pieces she brings.

"But it's all fine, right?" I finish. "I sent him options for new paintings and he can choose one and we'll be good to go."

I guess I'm worried because this is possibly my biggest show ever and we haven't heard back." Nova sighs.

"Can you give him what he wants?" Sierra asks. "Customer wants a Bud Light when we have perfectly good real beers on tap, I'll give it to them."

"You're comparing art to beer," I point out.

"Don't be a snob." She picks a sprinkle off her donut and tosses it at me.

I grin and catch it in my mouth. "Me? Hell no."

"Maybe I should have offered to paint something new for him. I could make it similar to the piece he wanted, in the style he liked so much."

"Don't do that," I plead. "He just needs time to adjust."

Nova nods slowly. "You're probably right. Enough work talk." Her expression brightens. "How are things with you and Miles since you moved back in?"

"Wait, back?" Sierra demands.

I catch her up on all of it, finishing with how I moved my things back in. Somehow, I managed to score an entire extra closet in the deal. Miles had already cleared it out for me, saying it was the only kind of "space" he wanted me to take.

Can't say he's not cute.

"I would've put money on the two of you a year ago," she sighs when I'm done. "There'd be ten of you in a booth, but I swear that man only looked at you."

"I mean…" I lift a shoulder in fake modesty.

"Oh, it went both ways." Sierra cuts my ego down to size.

I wave a hand in protest. "He fell harder. And first."

"Mile High's been crazy lately," she says when we stop laughing. "Lots of gossip and speculation about the team. And Miles." Sierra cuts a look my way.

I take a deep breath, deciding how much to confide.

In the end, I tell them all my suspicions, what we know.

"Do we need to start a murder board? With suspect photos and string?" Nova's expression brightens.

"Okay, Selena Gomez. There have been no murders in the Kodiaks's building, and there won't be. In fact, everything is going to be boring right up until playoffs."

"If we make it," Sierra says under her breath.

We finish our donuts in silence, staring at the furniture.

I can't solve Miles's mystery today, but I can help Nova.

"What if we angle the armchairs toward the couch? It could create a more inviting conversation area."

I notice a large, ornate armchair sitting awkwardly in the corner, out of scale with the rest of the room.

Suddenly, an idea strikes me. "We've been approaching this all wrong. We've been trying to force together pieces that don't quite fit."

Sierra looks at me, her brow furrowed. "What do you mean?"

I gesture to the armchair. "This armchair looks

out of place on its own. If we integrate it with the other pieces, it will make sense."

We implement the idea, and it's better.

Nova drops into the armchair with a relieved sigh. "Yes. That's it."

Sierra's phone rings, and she hops up. "Duty calls. Enjoy your day, ladies."

We hug her and wave her out before I sink onto the couch opposite, studying Nova. "I know Clay's parents visiting is a big deal, but work hasn't been the easiest either. I'm sorry for pushing you so hard about your new artistic style. We'll take it one step at a time, and I promise to help you find the right opportunities that will make it easier, not harder."

Nova returns my smile, her eyes shining with gratitude. "Thank you."

I pull her into a hug, feeling the last of the tension melt away. "That's what friends are for."

"You can take one more," Miles coaxes.

"I don't think so."

"Come on, Princess."

I hold up the line of thread, eyeing the multi-colored beads already on it.

The retirement home is having an activities afternoon, and we're making friendship bracelets with Miles's grams.

"Coco Chanel always said to take off the last thing you put on," Grams offers from her chair next to me.

"See? Thank you."

"What if this is the last thing you put on?" Miles holds out a bead with a heart on it.

It's cute. It would look pretty good with the pattern I've already made.

"Fine," I relent.

The lounge is full of residents and family members clustered around tables.

Some are making beaded accessories, others knitting, a few creating scrapbooks with photos and brightly colored paper.

"This is nice," I say.

"They have family activities every weekend," Grams says. "I like getting to meet new people and introducing them to Miles."

"You aren't ashamed of me?" Miles asks with a smile.

"Well, there was a pool going over whether you actually did it." Her whisper is conspiratorial, but her words set me back.

I'm not the only one. Miles stills, and it's only for a second, but it's enough that I know he's thinking about it.

"I hope you made some good money on it," I tease.

But I reach under the table and squeeze Miles's hand to let him know I've got him.

When I start to pull back, he holds on. His blue eyes are a thousand feet deep.

I could lose myself in this man.

I already have.

The past few days, the feelings are so big I could explode from them.

"Speaking of families"—she turns to me—"I see your mother on TV. I'm planning to vote for her."

"She'll be delighted to hear that," I say solemnly.

Grams leans toward me, lowering her voice. "But more than her, I have confidence in you. You're good for him you know."

My throat gets tight. I'm grateful to be spending this time with the woman who raised Miles. She's so supportive of him and welcoming of me.

Before I can respond, another lady calls Grams over to show her the scrapbook she's working on.

"She's really great," I tell Miles, my voice unusually rough.

"Yeah. I'm glad we moved her." Miles releases my hand and goes back to his work. "I'm guessing your mom isn't my biggest fan right now."

"It's not you." I recall her expression when I packed my things to return to Miles's, unsurprised and yet somehow disappointed. "It's her stubbornness. She thinks her way is the only way."

"She also wishes you were with some hotshot lawyer."

"You're a hotshot too," I tease.

"Hot shot bracelet maker you mean," he responds.

"Oh yeah? Let's see it, then."

He's been sneaky about his project, but now he holds it out.

I LOVE YOU BROOKE ELLIS.

My heart stops as I read the words spelled out in letter beads.

He's looking at me as though I'm everything that matters. "It's not Van Cleef or Cartier or whatever, but I thought you might like it."

I lean closer. "I love it."

Miles rubs a hand over his jaw. "Only the bracelet?"

I kiss him, and cheers go up.

19

MILES

HOOPSNEWS UPDATE: HAWKINS VOWS KODIAKS "DON'T STAND A CHANCE" IN MUST-WIN VERSUS BOSTON

"He's been running his mouth all week, saying how he's going to shut us down," Atlas grunts as we gather in the locker room.

Clay shakes his head. "Let him talk. We'll do our talking on the court."

A chorus of agreement rises from the team, a unified front against the looming challenge.

As the chatter continues, I slip away to my locker. The pregame jitters are there as always, but there's also a heaviness, a worry that gnaws at the pit of my stomach.

I reach into my bag, my fingers finding the edge of the photographs. I pull out the stack and stick them one by one up in my locker next to the picture of Brooke.

There's one of my guys after finals last year, another of me and Jay in college, plus a new one of Brooke and Grams from the retirement home yesterday with Brooke beaming and the blue bracelet I made her just visible on her wrist.

Yesterday, I told Brooke I loved her. It felt so damned good to get the words out after all this time.

But today, as I trace the lines of her smile, a chill of doubt snakes through me. The scandal, the rumors, and the speculation have been circling me like vultures, threatening to pick apart everything I've built.

What if I can't live up to what everyone expects of me? If I can't make the people I care most about proud?

I don't want this season to end. The Kodiaks need to make the playoffs and I'm going to get us there.

I owe it to the team, to myself, to be the man Brooke and Grams believe me to be.

"Miles, you ready for this?"

I turn to see Rookie, his eyes wide with a mix of nerves and excitement.

"Yeah." I clap him on the shoulder, mustering a smile. "Just stick to the plan."

As we gather, the energy in the room shifts. It's electric, a crackling current of determination and unity.

"All right," Jay says, his voice cutting through the tension. "This is it. There's no way around Hawkins, we've got to go through him.

"Boston thinks they have us beat. They think they can intimidate us, but they don't know what we're made of. They don't know the hours we've put in, the sweat we've left on this court. They don't know the heart of this team, but they're about to find out."

A ripple of energy passes through the room, a shared resolve that binds us together.

Coach claps his hands in agreement. "I want you to go out there and play your game. Play smart, play hard, play together."

His words wash over me, fueling the fire in my veins. I look at my teammates, seeing that same fire reflected in their eyes.

"Let's do this," I say, my voice ringing with conviction.

As we break the huddle, our hands joined in a unity circle, I push away the doubts and worries. This is where I belong. This is what I was meant to do.

We take the court to the roar of the crowd, adrenaline surging through my veins. Hawkins is there, his smirk already in place.

The ball goes up, and the game begins. It's time.

Boston's not here to fuck around.

They come out strong, their offense clicking with precision.

Hawkins is everywhere, his footwork impeccable as he weaves through our defense.

I'm playing great, but so is he. I grit my teeth, pushing myself harder with every play.

"Keep your head up, Garrett!" Coach barks from the sidelines. "Trust your teammates!"

I nod, forcing myself to take a deep breath. As we transition into offense, I see an opening. With a quick head fake, I drive toward the basket, drawing two defenders. At the last second, I dish the ball to Clay, who's wide open in the corner. He sinks the three, and the crowd erupts.

I barely have a moment to sneak a look up at the team box. Brooke and Nova are standing in their seats, holding onto one another as they watch intently.

The second quarter is when fatigue sets in. Am I

pushing too hard? Not hard enough? Hawkins seems to sense my inner turmoil.

"Heard you've been having some locker room issues, Garrett," he sneers during a free throw. "Maybe you should stick to partying in Vegas."

I clench my jaw, willing myself not to react, but the words fuel my fire. "Maybe you should worry more about basketball."

At halftime, we're down by seven. The locker room is tense, frustration palpable in the air. Coach's words wash over me, but I'm lost in my head, replaying every mistake, every missed opportunity.

"Miles?" Jay's voice cuts through my thoughts.

I look around at my teammates, seeing the trust in their eyes. They believe in me, even when I'm struggling to believe in myself.

The third quarter is a battle of wills. We claw our way back, point by point. A steal here, a clutch shot there. Rookie surprises everyone with a monstrous block on Hawkins, sending the crowd into a frenzy.

But Boston isn't going down without a fight. They match us shot for shot, their defense tightening like a vise. With every possession, the pressure mounts.

As we enter the fourth quarter, the score is tied. My muscles ache, sweat stinging my eyes, but I've never felt more alive. This is what it's all about. The challenge, the struggle, the chance to prove ourselves.

With three minutes left, Hawkins sinks a deep three, putting Boston up by two. The crowd goes silent, the tension almost unbearable.

Coach calls a timeout, gathering us close. "This is it, boys," he says, his voice steady. "Everything we've worked for comes down to these last few minutes."

His words settle over me, determination coursing through my veins.

As we retake the court, I catch Hawkins's eye. He's smirking, confident in his team's lead, but there's something else there too—a glimmer of respect, maybe even fear.

The ball is in my hands, the seconds ticking down on the clock.

Hawkins's taunts ring in my ears, his words like venom trying to seep into my veins. "Heard you're more interested in off-court drama these days, Garrett. How's that investigation going?"

I try to block him out, to focus on the game, but his jabs are relentless.

I feel my grip slipping, my feet stumbling.

But then, in the midst of the chaos, a voice cuts through. "Hey, Hawkins!" It's Jay, his eyes blazing with a fierce protectiveness. "Fans want to listen to you gabbing, they can tune into one of your podcasts instead of paying five hundred bucks for a ticket."

Hawkins sneers, but Jay isn't done. He turns to me, his hand firm on my shoulder. "Don't let this asshole get in your head."

His words hit me like a jolt of electricity. I look around, seeing the faces of my teammates, my brothers. They're nodding, their eyes filled with the same trust, the same belief.

A new resolve settles over me. "Let's do this."

As we start the next play, I feel a shift in the energy. We're moving as one, a united front against anything the world can throw at us.

The game resumes, and I'm seeing the court through new eyes. Every pass is crisp, every shot is true. We're clicking, our trust in each other translating into flawless execution.

Hawkins is getting more and more frustrated, his plays becoming sloppy and aggressive. He's trying to provoke me, to get a rise out of me, but I don't take the bait. I've got more important things to focus on.

The last three minutes tick by, the score climbing. We're neck and neck.

My gaze lifts to the crowd where Brooke's sitting. Her eyes, full of love and support, lock with mine.

I know I can do this. I can be clutch for my guys,

the team, the dreams of everyone who bet on this franchise.

The clock is winding down, mere seconds left. I've got the ball and a clear path to the basket. But out of the corner of my eye, I see Jay, open and ready.

I don't hesitate. With a flick of my wrist, the ball flies from my hands, a perfect arc across the court. Jay catches it, his eyes wide with surprise and gratitude. He jumps, the ball leaving his fingertips as the buzzer sounds.

The whole arena holds its breath. The ball seems to hang in the air for an eternity.

And then, with a satisfying swish, it drops through the net.

The crowd erupts, a deafening roar that shakes the very foundations of the building. My teammates are on Jay in an instant, their voices hoarse.

Over their heads, I catch a glimpse of Hawkins, his face twisted with disbelief and defeat, but he doesn't matter—not anymore.

20

BROOKE

The celebration at Mile High is a small reprieve from the looming playoffs. The team is crowded into booths, and I claimed a spot next to Miles.

"We did it!" Rookie crows.

"Sodas and water on the house," Sierra proclaims with a flourish, setting a tray on the table to hand out glasses.

"There you are," I say to Nova when she arrives, but my friend's expression is grim and at odds with the celebratory atmosphere. "What's wrong?"

She holds up her phone, and I take it to read the email message.

It's a note from Coastal Gallery saying they want to postpone the show. The don't even mention a date, just a statement that they'll "revisit later in the year."

My stomach plummets. "They can't cancel the show without cause. There's a cancellation fee if they do."

"But they didn't say cancel, they said postpone," she reminds me.

I pull up the agreement and read through. "I still don't see anything that would let them do that. Unless..." My heart sinks. "They can say we didn't deliver the pieces that were agreed to."

"Maybe I pushed too hard with the new pieces," Nova murmurs.

I can feel the disappointment rolling off my friend in waves.

"You didn't," I say quickly.

I pushed too hard.

What if I was trying to impress Nova, to advocate for her and prove I was capable?

I step outside for some air, my head spinning.

Helping the people I love matters more to me than managing my own brand. Which is why this failure hurts more.

"Wow, Brooke Ellis. I would've thought you'd do something different with your hair now that you're dating a celebrity."

The familiar voice slices into my thoughts.

Disbelief washes over me as I spin to face the alley. "Caroline?!"

My sorority sister closes the distance between us, her black wool coat flipped up at the collar against her white-blond hair.

"I debated whether to come to you about this. I wanted to leave you in the dirt, but I saw what happened to your boyfriend."

The surprise at seeing her is gone. "You mean you saw him and the rest of the Kodiaks crush Boston," I say.

"No," she says plainly. "I mean his recent downward spiral that's been spectacularly covered by the media." I'm about to shut her down when she continues. "I wanted to forget you ever existed, but Elise told me what you said about me in New York. That you did me a favor. So I'm about to do you one."

My protests die in my throat. I wait her out.

"I saw someone on the bench at the Kodiaks game a few weeks ago, a man who met with Kevin."

"Kevin," I echo, feeling a step slow. "Why would Kevin meet with someone on the Kodiaks?"

"There's only one reason—he thought he could use them." She lets that sink in a moment. "He wanted to get to Miles."

Kevin.

He was behind this.

My head is pounding. "Kevin tried to get Miles in trouble with the team... for revenge?"

"So, I haven't seen Kevin a lot lately, on account of the whole calling off the engagement thing." She shifts delicately on her feet. "But I did go to his offices to pick some of my things up, and he was already two drinks in. Turns out the trainer was supposed to get Miles's phone. Kevin thought he had pictures, evidence of something he'd done in school, but the trainer chickened out and didn't get the phone.

"Anyway, once the rumors went around about the drugs, he thought it would look like Miles was a victim if the phone was gone. So, Kevin figured it was working out better this way—Miles would be discredited, and anything he said would seem unreliable."

I'm trying to catch up, but there's an important piece missing.

"Do you know which trainer?"

Caroline laughs.

"Brooke, do you not remember when I memorized my entire economics course without attending half the classes on three hours of sleep after the Kappa spring mixer?" She blinks at me as if I'm being purposely dense. "I have a photographic memory. Of course I know which trainer."

The pieces are falling into place in my mind, a

plan taking shape. "I have to talk to the assistant trainer."

He might still be at the training facility. I can't exactly call him up and demand the truth, but I can surprise him in person.

Caroline grabs my arm as I move toward the door. "I'm going with you. We might not be friends, but Kappas don't let Kappas put themselves in that kind of danger."

I MAKE my excuses to Miles and the others at the bar. I say I'm tired, and he offers to come with me, but I insist I'm fine.

The drive to the arena passes in a blur of streetlights and nervous energy. By the time we pull into the parking lot, my palms are slick with sweat.

I throw the car in park in an empty spot with a view of the lot.

We sit there for five minutes. Ten.

"He's probably not coming," Caroline says.

"Thanks, Scooby Doo." There are still a couple of dozen cars with company parking passes—enough that I want to stick it out a bit longer.

She lifts a shoulder and pulls out a pack of almonds to snack on.

It's almost an hour before I spot the assistant trainer, heading toward his car. Taking a deep breath, I step out of my vehicle and call out to him. He freezes at the sound of my voice, his eyes darting around like a cornered animal's. As I approach, I see the sheen of sweat on his forehead, the tremor in his hands.

"Josh? We need to talk," I say, keeping my voice low and steady, "about the drugs you planted in Miles's locker."

His face goes pale. "I don't know what you're talking about," he stammers, but the lie is weak, transparent.

I press on, my heart racing. "We know it was you. We have a witness. But I also know you didn't do it of your own free will. Kevin Hildebrand put you up to it."

The trainer's eyes widen in shock and fear. "How... Who told you that?"

"It doesn't matter," I say. His reaction is as good as a confession. "What matters is that you have a choice now. You can come clean, help us expose Kevin for what he really is, or you can go down with him when this all comes out."

I see the conflict in his eyes, the war between fear and conscience. For a moment, I think I've gotten through to him. But then his phone chimes, and as he glances at the screen, swallowing hard.

"I-I can't," he chokes out, his voice trembling. "You don't understand. It's my family. I have to protect them."

My stomach drops.

He didn't do it for a payday. He did it out of fear.

"I'm sorry." Josh looks at me with desperate, pleading eyes. "I never wanted to hurt anyone, but I won't say anything else. Please, just leave me alone."

Before I can respond, he's fumbling with his car keys, practically diving into the vehicle. I watch him peel out of the parking lot, my mind reeling.

As I drag my feet back to the car, the weight of what's happened settles over me.

"What happened?" Caroline demands, opening the door to look at me over the top.

We were so close.

I lean against the car, suddenly exhausted. The cool metal against my forehead is the only thing that feels real in this moment of crushing defeat.

CAROLINE DROPS me off at Miles's condo when the phone vibrates.

Unknown number.

I click Decline. A moment later, it's ringing again. My heart pounds, a sense of foreboding settling over me. This time, I answer.

"Hello?"

"You think you're clever." Kevin's voice is sharp, cutting through the static. "I know you've been talking to people."

"Listen—"

"No, you listen." His tone is low, menacing. "You have no idea what you're getting yourself into, no idea what I'm capable of."

"What happened to being sorry?" I demand.

He chuckles. "I have regrets, Brooke, but that doesn't mean I don't also have plans."

My mind races. I knew his contrition was too good to be true.

"My family firm's donations form a big part of your mom's reelection campaign. If you don't back off, you're going to wish you had."

My heart hammers against my ribs. "Are you threatening me?"

"I'm saying that you have a lot at stake. You and your family."

The line goes dead.

21

BROOKE

"Princess. I was ready to send out a search party—"

"It was Kevin."

I walk in the door to see Miles getting up from the couch, Waffles tucked under one arm. "Huh?"

"Kevin was responsible for the drugs in your locker."

I fill him in on all of it—Caroline's help, the trainer. His expression hardens as I talk.

"Caroline said he thought you had proof of what happened back in college," I finish.

"I have photos of him in a pretty compromising position. But I'm not sure it's enough to bring him down today." Miles shakes his head. "He's a prick, but this is definitely another level."

In retrospect, it makes perfect sense. He thinks

Miles has details on his drug use from college and decides to use drugs to bring down the rival he hates.

"He called and threatened me. He wanted me to stop looking into it."

"What?" Miles is across the couch in a second. His hands find my arms, already tight with concern and simmering rage. "When I'm done with him, he won't be able to see fucking *anything*."

"No." I brush my palms over his face. "I'm fine, and you will get your team into the playoffs because that's your job. I don't need you fighting for me... unless it's with your words," I amend.

Miles groans, pulling me into his arms so tight it's hard to breathe.

"I don't like this, Princess."

"I know, but we don't have proof unless the trainer comes forward."

We sink back onto the couch, but neither of us is relaxed. He's perched on the edge, and so am I.

We brainstorm ideas, including going to the police, to my mom.

"She won't do anything," I say. "Kevin's family matters to her campaign. Even more if they're going through this big merger."

All night, he holds me.

The next morning, Miles has to go to practice. "Come with me," he says.

"I'll be fine."

"I don't like you being out here by yourself."

I try to push it from my mind when I go to work out.

When I shower.

When I take Waffles for a walk.

But anger surges through me, hot and fierce.

I see a post on social saying Kevin is accepting an ethics award on behalf of his family firm this week. In the photo, he's grinning, standing next to his grinning father and grandfather.

A sharp knock at the door jolts me. As I peer through the peephole, my breath catches in my throat. It's my mother, her face set in lines of grim determination.

The last thing I need right now is another lecture about staying out of this mess, but something in her expression gives me pause. With a deep breath, I open the door.

"What are you doing here?"

She steps inside, her eyes scanning the room before settling on me.

I brace myself for the familiar arguments, but as she takes a seat across from me, I notice something different in her demeanor. There's a tension in her shoulders, a glint in her eye that I've only seen when she's preparing for a major political battle.

"I owe you an apology," she says, catching me completely off guard. "I should have taken your concerns about Kevin more seriously. But I'm here now, and I want you to know that I'm on your side."

I stare at her, unsure if I've heard her correctly.

She reaches into her briefcase and pulls out a thick folder. "I've been doing a little digging of my own."

My heart races as she spreads documents across the coffee table.

I leaf through the papers, my mind reeling. "How did you find this?"

A small, grim smile plays at the corners of her mouth. "I didn't get where I am by playing nice. I have contacts, people who owe me favors. It didn't take long for the cracks to show."

I look at her, a mix of emotions churning in my gut: gratitude, hope, and a lingering thread of suspicion. "Why now?"

Her expression softens, a rare vulnerability shining through her political armor. "Miles came to my office. He reminded me about my responsibilities to you. I wanted to protect you, Brooke, but I didn't realize how bad it had gotten."

My mouth parts in shock. The sincerity in her voice brings unexpected tears to my eyes. "So, what do we do with all this?"

My mother's eyes harden, the seasoned politician taking charge. "Once this goes public, Kevin's family will have no choice but to cut him loose to save their own skins."

A surge of hope rises in my chest, but it's quickly tempered by worry. "Mom, this could destroy your campaign."

She takes my hand. "I've spent my entire career fighting for justice, for what's right, but I've never had a more important cause than protecting my daughter."

I squeeze her hand, overwhelmed. For years, I've felt as though I was fighting alone, even against my own family. Now, to have my mother not just on my side but leading the charge? It's almost too much to process.

As quickly as it appeared, her vulnerability is gone, replaced by steely determination. "We have work to do."

MILES

"Anyone still have legs?" Rookie groans as we head out of practice and back to the locker room.

"Coach didn't leave much of us to face Boston with," Damon agrees.

Two hours of hard drills had us on the floor. Thing is, our season will come down to Boston in the playoff game. It's our one chance at making it through.

We shower and change, the hot water making me feel slightly more human.

"I'm going crash hard," Jay says. "It's impossible to nap during the day because they're working on the house. But at night, I'm out cold."

Rookie looks and each of us. "You can't go home yet."

Jay finishes packing his bag and straightens. "Why not?"

"Movie night," he declares.

Normally, I'd be down, but it feels like the wrong time.

"We can't do a movie night. We have too much going on," I say.

"That's exactly why we should," he insists. "We need to remember what's at stake for us."

"Millions of dollars in contracts?" Atlas asks. "Sponsorships? Bragging rights?"

"No. I mean, yeah, but more than that." Rookie clears his throat. "It's our own belief in ourselves, you know?"

He expects us to laugh, but no one does.

"Nah, I think he's right," Jay decides.

I relent. "So, the big question: *Mighty Ducks* or *Little Giants*?"

An hour later, eight of us are taking up seats in Clay's home theater. The room in his new house was completely converted to provide terraced seating with chairs and three huge sectional sofas.

I'm leaning on my side on one, Jay taking up the other end.

We're a few minutes into the movie when my phone rings. The guys protest and throw popcorn at me as I step outside and answer. "Hey, Princess. Where are you?"

"Hi. I just got back to the condo. Mom and I went to talk. Thank you for getting her on board."

Her words have my spirits lifting. "I'm glad it worked." Dropping by the Senator's office was one of the easiest things I've ever done.

Not the getting in the door part, but the rest of it. I've wanted to tell to her exactly how incredible her daughter is, how she's blind if she doesn't see Brooke needs her, for a long time.

"See you in a couple hours?" I say. "We're all at Clay's watching *Little Giants*."

She chuckles. "You picked Devon Sawa over Joshua Jackson?"

"No way. Rick Moranis over Emilio Estevez. You jealous?"

"That you're watching that movie? Yeah. I think I might need a rewatch."

"You're going to drag your fancy ass over here to watch kids' movies? I'll believe that when I see it."

Half an hour later, the theater door swings wide. Brooke's standing there with Nova and Chloe and Sierra, their arms full of pillows and bags of snacks. The girls pile in, and we have to shift as they take up seats around us.

I pull Brooke between my legs. Chloe takes a chair on the other side of Jay.

"Are you crying?" Brooke asks her brother, kicking him lightly.

"You know I'm a sucker for the underdog," he says.

With everyone here, it feels like home—like family.

This is what it's all for.

We've got to face Boston in a couple of days.

But there's one more battle first.

22

BROOKE

The grand ballroom of the Four Seasons Hotel Denver glitters. Crystal chandeliers cast a warm glow over tables draped in pristine white linen, each place setting adorned with gleaming silverware and delicate china. The room buzzes with the quiet murmur of the legal world's elite, attorneys in impeccable suits, and politicians with plastered-on smiles.

I stand at the back of the room, my heart pounding. Caroline is beside me.

"You ready?" she whispers.

I nod, unable to trust my voice. We've been planning this moment, but now that it's here, I feel a flutter of doubt. What if we're wrong? What if no one believes us?

The host, a distinguished older woman with silver hair coiffed to perfection, takes the stage. "Ladies and gentlemen, it is my great pleasure to present this year's Lifetime Achievement Award for Excellence in Legal Ethics to the esteemed Hildebrand Law Firm, represented tonight by their rising star, Kevin Hildebrand."

A smattering of polite applause fills the room as Kevin strides to the podium, his smile dazzling under the spotlights. My fingers tighten around the folder in my hands.

Kevin's voice, dripping with false humility, booms through the speakers. "Thank you. It is truly an honor to accept this award on behalf of my family's firm. For three generations, our firm has stood as a beacon of integrity in the legal community."

I can't help but scoff, earning a few disapproving glances from nearby attendees.

"Ethics isn't just a word we throw around," Kevin continues, his chest puffed out with pride. "It's the very foundation of our practice. In a world where the line between right and wrong can sometimes blur, we've always strived to be on the right side of that line."

Caroline leans in close. "Now?"

I take a deep breath, steeling myself. "Now."

We move in unison, striding purposefully down the center aisle. Heads turn, whispers erupting in our wake. Kevin spots us, his eyes widening slightly before he recovers, seamlessly continuing his speech.

"I'm sorry to interrupt," I say, my voice ringing out clear and strong. "But there are some ethics we need to discuss."

A hush falls over the room.

Kevin's smile becomes strained, a bead of sweat forming on his brow. "Brooke and... Caroline. What an unexpected surprise. Perhaps we can chat after the ceremony?"

I shake my head, climbing the steps to the stage. "I'm afraid this can't wait, Kevin."

The host steps forward, clearly flustered. "I'm sorry, but this is highly irregular—"

"Please," I interject. "What we have to say is directly relevant to tonight's award. I promise you'll want to hear this."

I can see the curiosity warring with propriety on the host's face. After a moment, she nods, stepping back.

Kevin's eyes dart between us, a hint of panic creeping into his expression.

I turn to face the audience, my heart racing. "Ladies and gentlemen, I apologize for the disruption, but I couldn't stand by and watch this continue.

The firm you're honoring tonight is built on a foundation of lies, corruption, and flagrant disregard for the very ethics they claim to uphold."

A collective gasp ripples through the crowd. I see my mother sitting rigidly in her seat, her face a mask of calm support.

As Caroline sets up the computer, connecting it to the projector, I continue. "We've gathered evidence of numerous ethical violations. Bribes, witness tampering, destruction of evidence—the list goes on. Not to mention Mr. Hildebrand's history of cheating as far back as law school."

Kevin lunges for the microphone. "This is slander!"

But his protests are drowned out by murmurs as the first document appears on the screen behind us. It's an email chain, detailing a payoff to a key witness in a high-profile case. Kevin's name is clearly visible in the recipient list. I see shock, disbelief, and growing anger on the faces before me.

"This is just the tip of the iceberg," I say, my voice gaining strength. "We have financial records, sworn statements from former employees, even recorded conversations."

As Caroline cycles through the evidence, I watch Kevin. His face has gone ashen, eyes darting around the room like a cornered animal's. For a moment, I almost feel sorry for him—almost.

Kevin sputters, and his voice lacks conviction. "This is nothing but a desperate attempt to—"

"To what?" I interrupt. "To expose the truth?"

A distinguished man in the front row stands. "These allegations are extremely serious."

Kevin's composure finally cracks. "You don't understand. The pressure, the expectations... Do you have any idea what it's like trying to live up to the family name?"

I feel a surge of triumph, tempered by a strange sadness. "Yeah, I do. We all face pressure. We all have expectations to meet. But we choose how to respond to that pressure. You chose wrong over and over again."

Kevin slumps against the podium as the room explodes into chaos. Reporters are shouting questions, lawyers are huddled in intense discussions, and the awards host looks as if she might faint. Through it all, Caroline stands beside me.

"You did it," she murmurs, a hint of awe in her voice.

As security guards escort Kevin off the stage and the ethics committee members huddle in urgent conversation, I find myself scanning the crowd. I spot my mother, her face a mix of pride and concern. She gives me a small nod, and I nod back.

The host finally manages to restore some semblance of order. "In light of these... revelations," she says, her voice shaky, "the committee will need to reconvene to discuss the status of tonight's award. In the meantime, I think we could all use a moment to process what we've learned."

23

MILES

I stand offstage, my heart thudding in my back as I listen to the assistant trainer's trembling voice. The press conference room is packed, cameras flashing and reporters leaning forward, hanging on every word.

"I-I planted drugs in Miles Garrett's locker," Josh confesses, his voice barely above a whisper. "Miles is innocent."

The room erupts into chaos. Questions fly from every direction, but I can barely hear them over the roaring in my ears. Vindication fills me.

As it turned out, Josh's family had run into some problems with tuition and medical bills. We promised they would be protected if he came forward, and I offered my accountants to go over his finances and see if they could help.

Harlan steps up to the podium, his face a mask of controlled fury. "In light of this new evidence, Miles Garrett has been fully exonerated and any pending investigations fully suspended."

More shouting, more questions. I close my eyes, taking deep breaths. It's over. It's finally over.

I step up to the microphone, and the room falls silent.

"I want to thank everyone who stood by me during this difficult time," I say, my voice steady despite the emotion threatening to overwhelm me. "My teammates, my family. Your support meant everything." I pause, collecting my thoughts. "I'm grateful that the truth has come to light, and I'm glad to rejoin my team and focus on what matters most— winning games and bringing another championship to this city."

The questions come fast and furious: How does it feel to be exonerated? Am I ready for the playoffs?

I answer as best I can, but my mind is already on getting back to what I love.

As the press conference winds down, I feel a presence at my side. It's James, his expensive suit impeccable as always.

"Garrett," he says. "Glad things turned out the way they did. In fact, this whole comeback could play well for the team."

"Tell you what." I flash a grin. "You play whatever games you play upstairs. I just want to play ball."

I'm heading past the owner a few paces when my guys ambush me.

Rookie's first, engulfing me in a bear hug. "I knew you were innocent!" he cries, his enthusiasm infectious. "I told everyone who would listen!"

Atlas gives me a solemn fist bump.

Jay claps me on the back, his eyes shining with pride. "Welcome back."

Even Clay offers me a one-armed hug and a nod.

I take a deep breath, searching for the right words. "Thank you." My voice is thick with emotion. "For believing in me, for standing by me."

What happened made me realize how fragile all of this is, how quickly it can all be taken away. But it also showed me the strength of this team, of this brotherhood.

"Tomorrow, we're not just playing for a win. We're playing for each other. For every doubt we've overcome, every obstacle we've faced. We're playing to show the world what we're made of."

That's when I see Brooke standing at the back of the room. She's beautiful in a black dress, her hair pulled up on top of her head. Our eyes meet, and a thousand unspoken words pass between us. I make my way toward her, brushing off reporters with polite "no comments."

"You did it," she says when I reach her.

I shake my head. "*We* did it."

I scoop her up in my arms and spin her around. She laughs, her arms going around my neck.

"Couldn't have gotten through this without you," I murmur when I set her down.

"I'm sorry I brought Kevin to you."

"In a weird way, if it wasn't for him, I wouldn't have had the chance to be your fake date. Then your real date. Then your roommate."

"I am a pretty great roommate," she laughs. "Though I have some ideas for redecorating."

"Mmmm. We could go home and talk about them."

"Aren't you needed here?"

The buzzing activity behind me agrees with her.

"Nope. I'm all yours."

BROOKE

THE AROMA of freshly brewed coffee and artisanal pastries envelops me as I step into La Bohème. I scan the space, looking for the ideal spot.

There it is—a cozy nook near the back, bathed in natural light from a large window. The rustic wooden table is flanked by plush velvet armchairs in deep emerald green.

I'm settling into one of the chairs, pulling out my tablet when the bell above the door chimes.

Nova strides in, her pink hair twisted into a topknot. Her eyes light up when she spots me.

"Hey! This place is amazing," Nova gushes, sliding into the chair across from me.

"You found the last great café, so I owed you one."

"You said this was a work talk and not only a social talk. What did you want to meet about?"

I place both hands on the table. "So. I went back to the owner of Coastal Gallery and told him I screwed up. That you were willing to do a new floral painting for him if he wanted, and I advised you against it."

Nova's eyes widen. "You didn't have to do that."

"Yes, I did. I explained how important your new direction is to you. He was impressed at your willing-ness to create something new to fit his requirements, and said he'd give you another chance if you did."

Her breath whooshes out. "I'll think about it."

Surprise works through me. "Think about it," I echo. I expected her to jump at the chance, and I was ready to do everything in my power to make the show go off smoothly this time.

"Honestly, Brooke? I'm so grateful you did that, but while this has been going on, I'm getting more convinced that I want to move forward, not backward. Even though some people won't follow me in this new direction, that's okay. I'm going there anyway, for me and the people who will. I don't want to go backward."

"Okay then." I grin, relief spreading through my chest. I'm proud of my friend for making her own choices and standing up for herself. Either way, this will be her call and I'll have her back. "I also invited someone else to join us for coffee. You're going to kill me, but I wanted it to be a surprise because I didn't want you to stress about it."

Nova's excitement is palpable. "Who?"

I give her hand a reassuring squeeze.

The café's atmosphere seems to shift as Elise walks in. She's the epitome of effortless chic in a crisp white blazer over a silk camisole paired with tailored black trousers and sky-high stilettos.

"You didn't!" Nova hisses, recognizing the designer immediately.

"Just be yourself. You're a force of nature," I whisper back.

I stand to greet Elise, and Nova follows suit. "Elise, thank you so much for joining us."

Elise's smile is warm as she shakes my hand. "The pleasure is all mine." Her gaze shifts to Nova, and I see a spark of interest in her eyes. "And you must be Nova. I've heard wonderful things about you."

Nova's cheeks flush slightly as she shakes Elise's hand. "It's incredible to meet you. I'm a huge admirer."

Elise settles into the remaining chair.

We order our drinks—an almond milk latte for me, an espresso for Elise, and a chai tea for Nova.

"All right, ladies," I say. "While I genuinely wanted a chance for you two to meet, because you're both incredible artists with a unique vision, I'm not going to lie. I thought there might be room for a collaboration."

"Nova, why don't you tell me more about your art?" Elise prompts. "What excites you right now? Fashion is a seasonal industry, and while we try to create products that are as evergreen as possible, trends do matter."

Nova nods, sitting up straighter. "My new work is about color and space. I want to create pieces that make people feel confident, that tell a story."

Her confidence grows as she speaks, passion infusing every word.

Elise leans forward, engrossed.

As Nova delves into her new ideas for how to get her work to a broader audience—a series of limited-edition prints, collaborations with up-and-coming street artists, plans for a small clothing line—I watch Elise's reactions carefully. The fashion mogul's eyes sparkle with interest, and I can almost see the wheels turning in her head.

"These are fantastic ideas," Elise says. "What's holding you back?"

Nova hesitates, and I give her an encouraging nod. "Change is hard," she admits. "I have a loyal following, but gallery owners don't want me to deviate from what made me popular. I don't want to compromise my values or artistic integrity."

Elise nods thoughtfully. "I faced similar challenges when I was starting out. The key is to stay true to your vision while finding ways to make it accessible to a broader audience."

As Elise shares her insights, I find myself furiously scribbling notes. The conversation flows from challenges to solutions, from broad concepts to specific strategies. Before I know it, we're deep in a brainstorming session about potential collaborations between Nova and Elise's brand.

"This might be crazy, but I would love to see my art on garments. What if we did a limited-edition clothing line?" Nova suggests, her excitement palpable. "Something that combines your styles with my aesthetic?"

Elise nods enthusiastically. "I love that idea. We could do a capsule collection, maybe tied to a specific theme or cause, and we could amplify it with a coordinated social media campaign, leveraging both our platforms."

"Ooh, and what about pop-up events?" I chime in. "We could do simultaneous launches in key markets—New York, LA, London, Tokyo—make it a global event."

The energy at our table is electric as ideas bounce back and forth. Nova and Elise riff off each other, their different perspectives and experiences creating a perfect synergy.

As I help them flesh out the details of their ideas, I'm struck by how natural this feels. For so long, I struggled with my identity, trying to be something I thought others wanted me to be. Helping people I care about, whose visions I believe in, succeed is way more gratifying.

"Well," Elise says as the meeting winds down, glancing at her watch, "I hate to say it, but I have another appointment in half an hour."

Nova nods, a mix of excitement and nervousness on her face. "This has been incredible. I can't thank you enough for your time and insight, Elise."

"The pleasure was all mine," Elise replies warmly. "I haven't been this excited about a potential collaboration in years. Brooke, can I trust you to draw up a preliminary agreement for us to review?"

I nod, feeling a surge of pride. "Absolutely."

As we stand to say our goodbyes, Elise surprises us both by pulling Nova into a hug. "I have a feeling this is the beginning of something special."

After Elise leaves, Nova turns to me, her eyes shining. "Brooke, I can't believe that just happened."

I smile, wrapping an arm around her shoulders. "I can."

"But..." her face falls. "If this actually happens, it's going to be a lot of work. Do you have more hours to help me? I have more than enough money from my sales, and obviously, I'll compensate you like a publicist."

My chest squeezes. "As long as it doesn't get in the way of our friendship."

As we leave the café, stepping out into the April sunshine, I feel a sense of contentment wash over me. This is what I want to do, not for the fame or the money, but for moments like this—moments when I can help talented, passionate people connect and create something meaningful.

I may not be the one in the spotlight, but I'm finding my place.

WHEN I KNOCK on the door of Chloe's office, it takes her a second to glance up from her computer. "Look who it is."

She gestures to the chair opposite her desk.

I'm feeling more than a little guilt as I step inside and drop into the chair.

"I don't know if the offer's still on the table"—it's been almost a month since she put it out there—"but I'm going to have to decline it. I really appreciate you thinking of me and believing in me, because if I'm being honest, there are times when it's hard to believe in myself. But... long-term, I want to work for myself. So, I'm going to start building that even if it's hard."

"You're going to be an influencer again?"

I shake my head. "I'm going to run PR for Nova, and maybe I'll take on another few creatives if they're the right fit."

I recently heard back from Vivaro, who said they had completed their internal investigation and found no wrongdoing on their part. After emailing the group of women for whom I was speaking, I retained a lawyer and sent a letter outlining what was owed to the group. The influencers were paid out in less than twenty-four hours.

Two of the women have already asked if they can hire me to help them going forward.

Chloe's eyes sparkle.

"You're not mad," I read.

"No. I figured you would pass on the Kodiaks job, but giving you an opportunity here gave you a chance to think it over."

"How did you know I was agonizing over this?"

Her shoulder lifts. "Jay and I talk."

I lean forward in my seat, bridging my hands. "You do?"

There's been so much focus on my personal life lately that I'm not missing the chance to turn it around on somebody else—especially when those somebodies are my very private brother and the badass, professional woman who broke his heart when they were still kids.

Chloe folds her arms. "Occasionally."

"Occasionally, like, late at night you call him or he calls you? Or are these in-person conversations?"

She rises from her chair to walk me toward the door. "You need to go."

"Not at all, I've got all day." My grin is wide enough that Chloe shakes her head.

"Then *I* need to go."

She knocks the ID badge off her jacket, and we both bend to pick it up.

"You're not going to forget this are you?" she murmurs.

"Are you kidding? I need a new project, and I'll have you know I make an even better matchmaker than I do a publicist."

HOOPSNEWS UPDATE: DEFENDING CHAMPS DENVER FACE DOWN BOSTON FOR FINAL REMAINING PLAYOFF SLOT

24

MILES

The Visitors' locker room in Boston is quiet, each player lost in his own pregame ritual. I sit at my locker, staring at my jersey, tracing the familiar numbers with my fingers.

Rookie sidles up, his usual boundless energy tempered by nerves. "You think we can do this?"

I look at him, seeing the mix of hope and fear in his eyes. "I know we can."

Atlas grunts as he comes in and drops his bag at his locker. "What is it with Boston?!"

"What do you mean?"

"All their sports teams are tough. You wouldn't last a second in a Boston uniform," he informs Rookie.

Rookie shrugs. "My cousin got drafted to their hockey team. He's going to start next season."

A chorus of boos goes up around the locker room.

"He a nice kid like you? They'll chew him up and spit him out." Damon flashes teeth.

As game time approaches, the energy in the locker room builds. Coach gives his final speech, short and to the point. Then it's time. We line up and Jay turns to face us, his eyes blazing with intensity. "Who are we?"

"KODIAKS!" we roar back.

With a final battle cry, we run out into the stadium.

The crowd is a wall of sound and color.

It only makes us stronger.

As I run onto the court, I'm hit by a wave of emotion that nearly knocks me off my feet.

I made it. Despite everything, all the lies and betrayals and setbacks, I made it back here—to this moment, this team, this chance to earn our place in the playoffs and bring a series back to our home court in Denver.

As we take our places for tip-off, I look at my teammates. At Jay, our fearless leader. At Clay, a competitor to the core. At Rookie, brimming with potential. At Atlas, our silent strength. And I know, with a certainty that goes bone deep, that no matter what happens in this game or the ones that follow, we've already won—because we're here, together, ready to face whatever comes our way.

THE SQUEAK of sneakers on polished hardwood fills my ears. The crowd's roar is a distant hum, my focus laser-sharp on the task at hand. This is it. Winner goes to the playoffs, loser goes home. Everything we've worked for comes down to the next forty-eight minutes.

I glance at the scoreboard: 00:00. A fresh slate.

My gaze drifts to the stands, landing on Brooke. She's dressed in my jersey and standing with Nova and Mari and Chloe and...

Grams. My grandmother is here in Boston, wearing a Kodiaks jersey and beaming.

Brooke gives me a small nod, and I feel a surge of confidence. Win or lose, I know I'm not the same man who started this season.

Marcus Hawkins is across the court. He's smirking, cocky as ever. My blood boils, but it's not the same as when I thought he was fucking with us off the court.

This game, I know how to play.

The ref's whistle pierces the air. Tip-off.

Atlas wins the jump ball, tapping it back to me. I

pass it to Jay, setting the offense in motion, but something's off. Our passes are a beat too slow, our shots a hair too short. Boston's defense is suffocating, and before we know it, we're down 10-2.

Coach calls a timeout. We trudge to the bench, heads hanging low.

But it's Clay who drags us into the huddle, his tattooed arms urgent.

"Listen up," he says sharply. "We're not bottom feeders, we're defending champions. It's in our blood. In every one of us." Last year's Finals MVP nods to me, and it feels like an apology. "Now let's go out there and show them who the fuck we are."

His words light a fire in my chest. As we retake the court, I lock eyes with Jay. A silent understanding passes between us. It's time to turn this around.

The second quarter is a different story. We find our rhythm, chipping away at Boston's lead. Jay threads a no-look pass to Atlas for an easy layup. Rookie drains a three from the corner.

We're clawing our way back into the game.

With seconds left in the half, I drive hard to the basket. Hawkins steps up to challenge. I feel the contact, hear the whistle, see the ball drop through the net. The free throw brings us within two points at halftime.

In the locker room, the energy is electric. We can taste the comeback.

"We've got them on their heels," Coach says. "Now it's time to deliver the knockout punch. Clay, I want you running the pick-and-roll with Jay. Rookie, Atlas, be ready to crash the boards. Miles, keep that hot hand ready."

His words echo in my mind as we retake the court. The ball feels alive in my hands. We trade baskets with Boston, the lead changing hands with each possession. The crowd is on its feet, the noise deafening.

With two minutes left in the third, I see an opening. I fake left, go right, and drive hard to the hoop. Hawkins is there to meet me, but I'm ready. I leap, twisting in midair to avoid his block, and somehow manage to kiss the ball off the glass and in. The arena erupts.

The fourth quarter is a battle of wills. Every possession feels as though it could decide the game. With thirty seconds left, we're down by one. Coach calls our final timeout.

"All right, listen up," he says, his voice steady despite the tension. "We've got one shot at this. Miles, I want the ball in your hands. Everyone else, be ready. This is what we've practiced for. This is our moment."

As we break the huddle, Clay grabs my arm. "You've got this."

I nod, my throat too tight for words.

The inbound pass comes to me. I dribble, watching the clock tick down. Twenty seconds. Fifteen. Ten.

Hawkins is guarding me, his eyes burning with determination. I can almost hear his taunts from earlier in the season, but I'm not that Miles anymore.

Five seconds.

I make my move, driving right. Hawkins stays with me step for step. Three seconds. I pull up for the jumper, feeling Hawkins's hand graze my arm. The ball leaves my fingertips.

Time slows. The arena holds its breath. The ball arcs through the air.

Swish.

The buzzer sounds. For a moment, there's silence. Then the world explodes into noise. My teammates mob me, screaming in joy.

As the chaos swirls around me, I find myself face-to-face with Hawkins. There's no smirk now, just a look of grudging respect.

"Hell of a shot, Garrett," he says, extending his hand.

I shake it, feeling the last of our rivalry dissolve. "Hell of a game, Hawkins."

In the locker room, the celebration is wild. Jay's leading a chant, Rookie's dancing on a bench, and Clay's already talking strategy for the playoffs.

Coach quiets us down just long enough to say, "I'm proud of you boys. Now go enjoy this. You've earned it."

As the team files out, still buzzing with excitement, I linger. I sit on the bench, letting it all sink in. We're going to the playoffs. We have a shot at our second championship.

But more than that, I realize how far we've come, how far I've come. From the joker who didn't take anything seriously to the leader who just hit the biggest shot of his life.

A knock on the door interrupts my thoughts. It's Brooke, her eyes shining.

"That was some game, Garrett," she says, her voice soft.

I stand, crossing the room to her. "Couldn't have done it without you, Princess."

She laughs. "Pretty sure I wasn't the one who made that shot."

"Maybe not," I say, pulling her close. "But you made me the person who could."

As we leave the locker room hand in hand, I can't help but feel excited for what's to come. The playoffs await, another chapter in our journey, but whatever happens, I know I'm ready. We're ready.

25

BROOKE

ONE MONTH LATER

The sun beats down on the bustling charity sports event as I make my final checks. Clipboards, schedules, and a sea of volunteers in matching T-shirts surround me. I spot Miles weaving through the crowd, his tall frame and easy smile unmistakable even from a distance.

It's unseasonably warm for mid-May, and I send up a prayer of thanks. His Kodiaks T-shirt clings to the hard muscles of his shoulders and chest, and I let myself enjoy the view.

"There's my MVP," I call as he approaches.

"MVP of organization maybe." Miles grins, planting a quick kiss on my cheek.

My heart does a little flip. He still has that effect on me. "What are you talking about?! The Kodiaks crushed the first two rounds of the playoffs. You're into the conference finals."

Saying out loud only reinforces how proud I am of him. Of all the guys, really, including my brother. The team rallied and put together some stellar and gritty performances, and now they're playing like defending champions.

"We are pretty great," he concedes, a cocky expression taking over his face. He glances over my shoulder without releasing me from his strong arms. "This place looks amazing. You've outdone yourself."

I feel a flush of pride. "Well, since I passed on working for Chloe, I offered to help out today. Speaking of which, where's our furry mascot?"

Right on cue, a whirlwind of fawn-colored fur comes barreling toward us, tongue lolling and stub of a tail wagging furiously. Waffles skids to a halt at our feet.

Miles laughs, scooping him up. "Ready to charm some donors?"

I check my watch. "And just in time. We're due to kick things off in five."

We make our way to the makeshift stage, Waffles trotting happily beside us. As we climb the steps, I feel a familiar twinge of nerves.

"Ladies and gentlemen," the announcer's voice

booms, "please welcome Miles Garrett and Brooke Ellis!"

The crowd erupts in cheers and applause. I take a deep breath, squeezing Miles's hand before stepping up to the microphone.

"Welcome, everyone, to the Hoops for Hope charity event!" My voice carries across the crowd. "We're thrilled to see so many familiar faces and new friends here today. Your support means the world to us."

Miles steps forward, his presence reassuring. "Every dollar, every shot, every cheer today goes toward building a brighter future for kids in need. So, let's make some noise and have some fun!"

The crowd roars its approval.

As we make our way down from the stage, we're swept up in a whirlwind of activity. Fans clamor for autographs, reporters shout questions, and somewhere in the chaos, Waffles decides it's the perfect time for an impromptu game of chase.

"Waffles, no!" I laugh, watching the little bulldozer weave through a forest of legs.

Miles is hot on Waffles's tail, calling out apologies as he goes.

I turn to find a microphone in my face, attached to an eager-looking reporter. "Ms. Ellis, how does it feel to be here today given the recent turbulence in your personal and professional life?"

For a moment, I'm taken aback. I shouldn't be surprised they're bringing up what happened with Kevin, but I've learned from it, grown from it. I meet the reporter's gaze steadily.

"It feels incredible," I say, my voice strong and clear. "Life throws curveballs, but it's how we handle them that defines us. Today is about moving forward, about using our experiences to make a positive impact."

I catch sight of Miles returning, Waffles tucked securely under one arm. He gives me a wink, and I can't help but smile.

The fallout from Kevin's exposure has been nothing short of seismic. What started as Miles and me taking a stand against injustice quickly snowballed into a scandal that's shaken the legal community to its core.

Kevin's family firm, once a beacon of legal prestige, has been forced to dissolve. The ethics violations were too egregious to ignore, and the bar association's swift action was both necessary and unprecedented.

But the revelations didn't stop there. A full investigation uncovered a pattern of academic fraud stretching back to Kevin's college days. Adding

Miles's photos of Kevin's dorm room drug stash felt like overkill. He's facing a raft of legal charges that will take time to work through the system, but in the meantime, the disbarment as well as revocation of his law degree feel like fitting blows.

The consequences have struck close to home, too. My mom's campaign took a significant hit thanks to the loss of Kevin's family as major donors. But her team is nothing if not resilient. They're trying to reframe the narrative around integrity and standing up against corruption.

Lately, they seem to think she might actually come out ahead for taking a stand against unethical behavior, even at great personal and professional cost.

I hope she does.

The reporter moves on, and Miles sidles up beside me. "Ready to show them some real teamwork?"

I grin, competitive spirit flaring. "Bring it on, hotshot."

We head to the first challenge—a shoot-out. The rules are simple: sink more baskets than your competition in one minute. Miles, naturally, will be in his element, but I've picked up a thing or two over the years.

"Ladies first," Miles teases, handing me a ball.

I quirk an eyebrow. "Careful what you wish for."

The whistle blows, and we're off. I sink my first shot, then my second. Miles matches me basket for basket, his form perfect, his concentration intense. But I'm no slouch either. As the seconds tick down, we're neck and neck.

"Ten seconds!" the announcer calls.

I grab my last ball, take a breath, and let it fly. It arcs through the air, then... swish! Nothing but net.

The buzzer sounds, and the crowd goes wild. Miles sweeps me into a bear hug, lifting me off my feet.

"Unbelievable!" He laughs. "You ever want to retire from PR, you have another career waiting, Princess."

As we catch our breath, I spot a familiar face making its way through the crowd. My brother, decked out in event gear, grins as he approaches.

"Not bad," he says, clapping Miles on the back.

"Jay!" I pull him into a hug. "I thought you weren't getting here until later."

He shrugs. "Couldn't miss my little sister showing up the pros. Plus, I heard there's a relay race that needs a third wheel."

Miles chuckles. "More like a secret weapon. You in?"

Before Jay can answer, there's a commotion from

the autograph tent. I spot Waffles darting between tables, a string of fans in pursuit.

"Oh no," I groan. "I thought we had him secured."

"I got this," Miles says, already moving. "You two head to the relay. I'll meet you there."

As Miles disappears into the crowd, I can't help but marvel at how different things are now. A year ago, I wouldn't have trusted anyone else to handle a crisis, big or small, but Miles has shown me that I'm not alone anymore.

"Earth to Brooke." Jay's voice cuts through my thoughts. "You good?"

I nod, smiling. "Yeah, just... reflecting."

Jay's expression softens. "It's good to see you happy."

"Even if I'm with Miles?"

He grins, rolling his eyes. "Yeah. I'm sorry I was a dick about it. I've never seen him care about anyone the way he cares about you, and once I realized that, I knew I'd square with it." He folds his arms. "This way, I can keep an eye on both of you. And if someone's dodging my texts, I'll find out."

I'm still laughing as Miles jogs up, slightly out of breath but grinning triumphantly. "Crisis averted. Waffles is now the proud owner of about fifty new toys from the merch tent."

I laugh, shaking my head. "My hero."

"Penny for your thoughts?" he asks when we're both quiet a moment.

I take a deep breath. "I was just thinking about how far we've come, how much we've both changed."

He nods, understanding in his eyes. "For the better, I hope?"

"Definitely," I say softly. "I never thought I'd trust someone like this. But you've shown me what real partnership looks like."

Miles takes my hand, his touch gentle. "I used to think being friends with everyone was safer, easier. I didn't have to risk being really close to anyone. But what we have? It's worth every challenge, every risk."

Tears prick the corners of my eyes. "Even when I'm being stubborn and independent?"

He chuckles. "Especially then. Your strength is one of the things I love most about you. I don't want to change you. I just want to be the person you can lean on when you need to."

I lean in, resting my forehead against his. "I love you, Miles Garrett."

"I love you too, Brooke Ellis," he murmurs. "Now, what would you say to a hot air balloon ride?"

I spin around, searching the horizon. "You didn't."

"I know how you love adventure. And looking

down at all the little people," he teases, reminding me of the sorority retreat.

I slap his arm lightly and he pulls me against him into a hard kiss.

Yes. This is everything I want.

The jokes and the earnestness. The heat and the sweetness. The dreams and the reality.

Waffles is exhausted from his day of mischief making, so we leave him snoozing with my brother and make our way hand in hand to the setup for the hot air balloons.

"Ready for this, Princess?" Miles asks, eyes sparkling with excitement.

I grin. "Never."

I lean against Miles, content in a way I never thought possible.

"So," he says, his voice soft, "think we make a good team?"

I smile, thinking of all we've been through, all we've overcome. "The best."

EPILOGUE
FOUR MONTHS LATER

Kevin sits in the cold, sterile lecture hall, his stomach churning with a mixture of anger and humiliation. The faces looking back at him are young, eager, and untainted by the harsh realities of the legal world.

How he envies their naïveté.

"Welcome to Legal Ethics 101," he says, his voice flat and lifeless. "I'm here to tell you a cautionary tale. A story of ambition, corruption, and the steep price of losing one's way."

As he launches into his court-mandated lecture, Kevin can't help but marvel at the cruel twist of fate. Instead of serving time behind bars, he was sentenced to relive his misdeeds, to expose his shame to the bright-eyed idealists who represent everything he once was.

Each word tastes like ash in his mouth, but he forces himself to continue. He speaks of the allure of power, the seductive whisper of greed. He recounts the moment he crossed the line, the first compromise that set him on a path of no return.

"It starts small," he warns, his voice taking on a haunted edge. "A little white lie here, a bent rule there. But before you know it, you're so far gone that you can't even recognize yourself in the mirror."

The students listen, some with rapt attention, others with a mix of pity and revulsion. Kevin sees the wheels turning in their heads, each one convinced they could never fall prey to the same temptations.

If only they knew.

As the lecture draws to a close, Kevin feels a wave of exhaustion wash over him. This is his penance, his cross to bear, and he will carry it for as long as the court deems necessary, a living testament to the dangers of unchecked ambition.

BROOKE

"WE'RE OUT OF BEER," Damon hollers.

My brother's house erupts in a chorus of dismayed protest.

"Outside," Sierra corrects, shooting him a look. "You're out of beer *outside*." She gestures to the neat stack of cases in the corner.

The kitchen at Jay's house is bustling and packed with bodies. I'm surrounded by the familiar chaos of holiday preparations for the Labor Day BBQ.

"If you're here, who's on the grill?" Jay leans over the island toward his teammate.

Damon lifts the apron off his head. "Atlas."

"Atlas can't grill."

"Dude, this is my first summer here. How the hell am I supposed to know that?!"

A plume of smoke drifts across the window. "Fuck."

"On it!" Nova says, dashing toward the door in a blur of denim, her pink ponytail bouncing.

"Bet you didn't think you'd need twenty-four champagne glasses," I say to my brother.

"You did."

That's why I got them for his housewarming.

"Who are we missing?" I'm pouring the twentieth glass from the fifth bottle of Dom and scanning the open-concept area critically.

Most of the team is here, minus the guys traveling for the holiday.

My parents are here too, and Miles's grams, plus Nova's sister and brother-in-law, Harlan. They're all sitting around the living room, talking eagerly. Mom's smiling her genuine smile, not the campaigning one.

"Rookie."

The sound of the door closing has us looking up.

"My name is Ryan," he calls. "We went through this last year."

"When you sign a new contract, we will stop calling your Rookie," Jay says.

He pulls out his phone with a flourish. "It's done, assholes!"

The guys all holler their congratulations.

The warm, comforting scents of the grill fill the air, mingling with the laughter and chatter of the Kodiaks.

My eyes are drawn to Miles, who looks extra hot in dark jeans and a dress shirt that matches his eyes.

As sexy as he is, he seems fidgety. He's standing by the counter, his hand constantly dipping into his pocket as if checking for something.

"Tell me you're not stressing about the games again." I arch a brow. "They're months away."

His new goal is to make the national team next year, and he's devoted himself to an extra-rigorous training regimen to make it happen.

He flashes me a grin. "Nah, it's not that."

"Well, you're definitely distracted. Which means you must be reliving the way we celebrated after your last game of the season."

His eyes glint wickedly. "Now I sure as fuck am."

I feel myself flush as he steps behind me, resting a hand lightly on my waist. I love the way he touches me, and the fact that we can do it in public without having to hide it anymore. "But that's not it, either. You need a hand?"

"You can help by passing these out." I wave to the champagne flutes, and he obligingly distributes them.

Once everyone has a glass, my brother gives a toast to the team.

"Because winning a championship is hard but running it back is harder. To the Kodiaks family."

We all drink.

As I move around the kitchen, helping Jay with the last-minute details, I feel Miles's presence beside me. His hand finds mine beneath the table, and he leans in close.

"Can I steal you away for a moment?" he whispers, his breath warm against my ear.

Curiosity piqued, I nod and allow him to lead me into the hallway.

Miles takes a deep breath, emotion rolling off him in waves. "From the moment I met you, I knew my life would never be the same. You've been my rock, my guiding light through the darkest of times. Your strength, your compassion, your unwavering belief in me... it's everything."

Tears spring to my eyes as I'm overwhelmed by the depth of his words. My hand tightens around his, anchoring myself in this moment.

"I can't imagine my life without you," Miles continues, and suddenly he's dropping to one knee. My heart leaps into my throat. "You make me want to be better, even when things are hard. And I want to spend the rest of my days proving myself worthy of your love." With trembling hands, he pulls out a small velvet box and opens it, revealing a stunning diamond ring. "Brooke Ellis, will you marry me?"

For a moment, I'm frozen, overcome with emotion. Through my tears, I find my voice. "Yes," I whisper, nodding emphatically. "Yes, I will."

As he slips the ring onto my finger, a sense of rightness washes over me. This is where I belong— by Miles's side, ready to face whatever life throws our way.

Hand in hand, we return to the dining room, our faces glowing with joy. My family and our friends erupt in cheers and congratulations when they notice the ring. Miles pulls me close, and I melt into his embrace.

"I love you," he murmurs, pressing a soft kiss to my temple. "I want to do everything with you—in public and in private. I booked us an island trip where we can go surfing and swim with dolphins and do all the things we talked about."

My chest squeezes, but it's the best feeling in the world.

"I love you too," I reply, my eyes shining with the promise of our future together.

As the celebration swirls around us, I know that this is just the beginning. A new chapter in our story, one filled with love, laughter, and the unshakable bond we've forged through adversity.

Together, we're ready for anything.

Thank you for reading *Hard to Break*! Miles and Brooke have etched a place in my heart, and I hope you love them as much as I do.

Hungry for more Kodiaks? Visit my website to download a special holiday story featuring Miles, Brooke, and the entire team celebrating the season— complete with a few surprises!

Last but not least: Clay and Nova's addictive,

enthralling complete story is available now in the
King of the Court series.

Love,

Piper

~

For writing updates, early excerpts and exclusive
giveaways...
Join my VIP List and never miss a thing!
www.piperlawsonbooks.com/subscribe

BOOKS BY PIPER LAWSON

DENVER KODIAKS SERIES

It's not every day you ask your older brother's teammate to be your fake boyfriend. But desperate times call for gorgeous, impulsive measures.

Denver Kodiaks is a steamy, brother's teammate sports romance about a sorority reunion, a college crush, and a love that's bigger than basketball.

KING OF THE COURT SERIES

After being dumped and losing my job the same week, the last thing my broken heart needs is a rebound.

A steamy, grumpy sunshine sports romance featuring a woman down on her luck, a star basketball player with a filthy mouth, and a connection neither of them can deny.

OFF-LIMITS SERIES

Turns out the beautiful man from the club is my new professor... But he wasn't when he kissed me.

Off-Limits is a forbidden age gap college romance series. Find out what happens when the beautiful man from the club is Olivia's hot new professor.

WICKED SERIES

Rockstars don't chase college students. But Jax Jamieson never followed the rules.

Wicked is a new adult rock star series full of nerdy girls, hot rock stars, pet skunks, and ensemble casts you'll want to be friends with forever.

RIVALS SERIES

At seventeen, I offered Tyler Adams my home, my life, my heart. He stole them all.

Rivals is an angsty new adult series. Fans of forbidden romance, enemies to lovers, friends to lovers, and rock star romance will love these books.

ENEMIES SERIES

I sold my soul to a man I hate. Now, he owns me.

Enemies is an enthralling, explosive romance about an American DJ and a British billionaire. If you like wealthy, royal alpha males, enemies to lovers, travel or sexy romance, this series is for you!

TRAVESTY SERIES

My best friend's brother grew up. Hot.

Travesty is a steamy romance series following best friends who start a fashion label from NYC to LA. It contains best friends brother, second chances, enemies to lovers, opposites attract and friends to lovers stories. If you like sexy, sassy romances, you'll love this series.

PLAY SERIES

I know what I want. It's not Max Donovan. To hell with his money, his gaming empire, and his joystick.

Play is an addictive series of standalone romances with slow burn tension, delicious banter, office romance and unforgettable characters. If you like smart, quirky, steamy enemies-to-lovers, contemporary romance, you'll love Play.

MODERN ROMANCE SERIES

When your rich, handsome best friend asks you to be his fake girlfriend? Say no.

Modern Romance is a smart, sexy series of contemporary romances following a set of female friends running a relationship marketing company in NYC. If you enjoy hot guys who treat their families like gold, fun antics, dirty talk, real characters, steamy scenes, badass heroines and smart banter, you'll love the Modern Romance series.

ABOUT THE AUTHOR

Piper Lawson is a *Wall Street Journal* and *USA Today* bestselling author of smart and steamy romance.

She writes women who follow their dreams, best friends who know your dirty secrets and love you anyway, and complex heroes you'll fall hard for.

Piper lives in Canada with her tall and brilliant husband. She's a sucker for dark eyes, dark coffee, and dark chocolate.

For a complete reading list, visit
www.piperlawsonbooks.com/books

Subscribe to Piper's VIP email list
www.piperlawsonbooks.com/subscribe

amazon.com/author/piperlawson

bookbub.com/authors/piper-lawson

instagram.com/piperlawsonbooks

tiktok.com/@piperlawsonbooks

facebook.com/piperlawsonbooks

goodreads.com/piperlawson

ACKNOWLEDGMENTS

Thank you for reading *Hard to Break*! I hope you've loved Miles and Brooke's steamy, fun, and a little twisty best friend's brother story.

This book wouldn't have happened without the support of my awesome readers, including my ARC readers. Thank you for providing endless enthusiasm, cheerleading, early feedback, and help spreading the word.

Becca Mysoor: It blows my mind how many good ideas you have on the regular. Thank you for being such an inspiration and overall smart cookie.

Cassie Robertson: I'm amazed you still let me slide into your calendar after all these years. Someday, I'll write a scene with blocking on the first pass. (Fine, the second.)

Devon Burke: I hate the thought of writing a book

without having you to catch my typos and show biz faux pas. (Is that how you write that? I'm adding this note after you read the book, so we'll never know.)

Annette Brignac: You are the first person with a stunning mockup for cover reveal day and a paper bag for hyperventilating on "why the hell did I decide to write this book?!" day. I am in awe of you.

Kate Tilton: You do the things I should be doing, and you do them better than I would. Thank you for making my life better.

Lori Jackson and Emily Wittig: You take my random ideas and wacky gradients and making art from them. Thank you for responding to my emails when I ask for one more tweak three months after you've forgotten who I am.

Georgana Grinstead, Kim, Christina, Sarah, Jos, and the entire VPR team: You make the complicated work of publishing seem effortless. Thank you for your wisdom, genius, and tireless effort to help readers find books they'll love.

Last but not least, thank YOU for reading. Truly.

Knowing we're living in these words and worlds together is the best part of any gig I've ever had.

Love always,

Piper

www.ingramcontent.com/pod-product-compliance
Lightning Source LLC
Chambersburg PA
CBHW061120310726
48974CB00002B/615